Zeke's Reluctant Omega

Draco International #3

An MM/MPreg Shifter Romance

I0533157

by

A.J. Stone

Zeke's Reluctant Omega (Draco International 3)
Copyright © November 2018 by A.J. Stone
Print ISBN: 978-1-942414-54-4

Editor: Nicoline Tiernan
Cover Artist: Nic T.

Published by Lost Goddess Publishing LLC

This book is a work of fiction. While reference might be made to actual historical events or existing locations, the names, characters, places and incidents are either the product of the author's imagination or are used fictitiously, and any resemblance to actual persons, living or dead, business establishments, events, or locales is entirely coincidental.

Warning: This book contains sexually explicit scenes and adult language and may be considered offensive to some readers. It is not meant for underage readers.

About Zeke's Reluctant Omega

As Head of Security for Draco International, Ezekiel Lowry is the unofficial fixer for the company. When a fellow dragon shifter unintentionally almost kills someone, Zeke is in charge of damage control. The moment he sets eyes on the victim, he knows he's looking at the man who will become his omega.

Marcel Yardan moved to Verdance to pursue a career as a dancer. When an accident ruins his big stage debut, Marcel finds himself bitter and blaming the man sent to make sure he doesn't sue Draco International—even though his canine whimpers and whines for the handsome alpha shifter. Nothing about Zeke fits with Marcel's life plan.

Pushing away the alpha who makes his heart pound is a risky move, but when Marcel spies Zeke with another omega, his world comes crashing down—again.

Welcome to Draco International, home of high-powered dragon shifters who live by their own rules. This 41,000-word MPreg novel includes passionate and explicit sexual content, as well as some violence. Suitable for adult audiences.

Chapter 1

Marcel

Excitement fluttered through Marcel, a butterfly weaving drunkenly from his stomach to his throat and back down. Each brush of wing against his heart made it beat erratically. He inhaled through his nose and exhaled through his mouth in a vain attempt to control his rocketing emotions.

He'd arrived.

Not figuratively, the way he planned, but literally, which was the first rung on his ladder to success.

Being in Verdance meant he'd taken the most difficult and drastic step in kickstarting his career as a leading man of the theater. He'd walked away from law school and his parents' lifelong dream that he become an attorney. Marcel had stars in his eyes, and every one of them had his name emblazoned on it.

The bus stopped, and most of the riders disembarked, their legs slowly stretching as people worked out kinks and cramps from sitting for so many hours. Moans, of the pained and pleasured variety, accompanied the raising of arms and arching of torsos as people waited for the driver to open the storage compartment so they could retrieve their bags.

Marcel bypassed the crowd. He'd brought a single backpack full of everything he needed to sustain himself until he landed that coveted leading man role. He checked the time on his phone, and then he tucked it into his pocket. There was just enough time to make it to his scheduled audition for a part in *Dance of the Dragons*, a promising new musical being launched in this fine city. Marcel planned to be part of the original cast.

This was his ticket to Broadway—and beyond. London. Paris. Sydney.

The theater scene in Verdance was top-notch, the largest and most prestigious community of players in a thousand miles. Perhaps it was miniscule when compared to what was happening on the East or West Coasts—Verdance was a small town when compared with Los Angeles or New York—but it was a noteworthy place to start.

Jason Sharp had started out in Verdance. Seeing the star perform had changed Marcel's life, and when Sharp had taught a summer theater program in Marcel's small town for two summers in a row, Marcel had signed up both times. He'd studied Sharp's techniques while absorbing everything about his life. Sharp had started out starring in an original stage production in Verdance, and he'd been discovered by a big name producer. He'd even been an understudy for one of the main characters in *Hideout*, a production that was still sold out all over the world. Marcel couldn't remember the particular part Sharp had played, but he didn't care. He didn't plan to follow in Sharp's exact footsteps.

The idol's path provided a blueprint for Marcel to modify to fit his goals. Sharp had peaked too soon. Marcel's star was going to soar even higher than his mentor's.

Stopping off in a public restroom at a park next to the theater, Marcel checked his reflection and grimaced. He did not travel well. The motion of the coach made his stomach queasy, and he hadn't eaten since dinner the day before. He combed his hair and used styling gel to help define and prop up his tight curls. The height brought out his eyes and took some of the emphasis away from his nose, which was a little too large and angular for his almost angelic features.

He kind of looked like he'd broken his nose when he'd fallen to Earth from Heaven. Of course, he'd broken it when he'd fought Vinnie Brown for hurling homophobic slurs in Marcel's direction. Yes, Marcel could double as a faerie prince, but he was a scrappy one. Marcel had come out of the fight with a hook to his nose, the result of the one punch Vinnie had landed, and the prejudiced bad guy had ended up needing twelve stitches on his face and casts on his arm and foot.

Dog shifters had a wickedly strong set of jaws, and Marcel knew how to fight. Years of playing around with his littermates meant he could both take and throw a punch. He kept his wits about him in life-threatening situations, and he wasn't afraid to use his hard head or his sharp elbows. Brown had missed six days of school, and when he'd returned, he'd avoided Marcel, even going so far as to change two of his classes.

Nobody messed with Marcel after that. He might have an effeminate beauty, but he wasn't at all wimpy.

With his hair looking perfect, Marcel changed into his leotard. Bright colors cut through the mostly black fabric to emphasize his muscular legs and butt. The shirt was looser, with flowing arms that enhanced his gracefulness.

Then he made up his face, disappearing all signs of travel fatigue.

Adrenaline rushed through his veins. Today was the first day of the rest of his life.

The theatre was much smaller than Marcel had anticipated. It occupied half of the building, with the other half being a coffee shop, a leather goods store, an appliance store, and a pet supply store. The unlit marquee advertised a weekend run for *All the Wrong Reasons*. A smaller sign posted on the door indicated that auditions for *Dance of the Dragons* was going on at that moment.

Marcel went inside. The lobby was chic and modern, the chrome and marble theme not aspiring even a little bit to imitate classic architecture. The city of Verdance was quite old, but this part of town seemed shiny and new. His community college auditorium, mired in the 1960's décor, seemed far more theatrical by comparison.

"Are you here to audition?" A middle-aged man with a polite, plastic smile came out from the box office.

Summoning his brightest smile, Marcel said, "I am. I have an appointment."

The man waved his hand toward the rear of the lobby. "Through those doors. You'll see Scylla inside. Tell him who you are, and then have a seat. They'll call you when they're ready."

A pair of men came in behind Marcel, and as he headed into the theater, he heard them tell the man they were walk-ins, and they were directed to the same place as Marcel.

Marcel forced his brief frown away, and he summoned hope from his natural well of internal sunshine. This was his day. He was going to walk out of there with the lead—or, at least, having wowed them enough for a juicy role.

Scylla was a barrel of a man squeezed into tight sweats and a coffee-stained shirt that could not contain the entirety of his bulk. He smelled slightly of the sea, which was odd because the ocean was even farther away in Verdance than Marcel's hometown. Marcel's nose twitched as it analyzed the mustiness and brine. Sometimes being a canine shifter had drawbacks. He was sure the humans here didn't notice Scylla's fishy odor.

Folders and papers were strewn over the table where Scylla sat, though his attention was divided between the man singing onstage and whatever was on the screen of his laptop. The guy onstage was pretty good, and with his deep baritone, he was going for a different part than Marcel.

Scylla stood when Marcel approached. "What's your name, son?"

Marcel smiled. "Marcel."

Scylla waited, and when Marcel didn't continue, he prompted, "Last name?"

"No last name. I'm simply Marcel." Another component to Marcel's quest for fame and theatrical success was the adherence to the idea of a single name. All of the greats could be recognized using one name—Liza, Madonna, Picasso.

Scylla seemed unfazed. "I have a Marcel Yardan."

With a sigh, Marcel claimed the name. While he loved his family, Yardan was not a sexy name, and so it had to go.

The barrel-man handed over a sheet of paper. "Lines, part of a song. On the back is the audition timeline. Today are initial looks. Callbacks will be posted tonight at eight." He pointed to a group of men sitting in the middle of the center rows of seats. "Sit there. The director will call you when she's ready."

The gaggle of hopefuls sat silently. Marcel had always pictured his pre-audition time as being one where he stretched and practiced vocal exercises. He didn't think he'd be sitting quietly, waiting for his group to be called. And so he used his ability to make subsonic sounds to practice his lines in a way the others couldn't hear.

It didn't take long for him to be called to the stage. He delivered his lines and sang along with the pianist, and then he performed a short version of the dance he'd done in the recital for his hip-hop class six years ago.

An hour after arriving, he found himself on the street with five hours to wait until the callback sheet was posted.

Eight o'clock found him waiting impatiently outside the theater in a crowd of hopefuls. Eight-oh-seven featured him pirouetting on the sidewalk. Listed under dancer and chorus was his full name, not the single-word title he preferred. No matter—a callback was a callback. He was one step closer to achieving his dream.

Now he needed to find a place to sleep for the night.

It didn't take long for him to establish that Verdance featured expensive hotels. If he stayed in one for even a few days, his cash stores would be depleted—and there was no way he was going to ask his parents for help. They didn't approve of his pursuit of a career in theater. Though they spoke to him, they still hadn't forgiven him for dropping out of college and refusing to attend law school.

As staying in a hotel wasn't feasible, Marcel went looking for other options. He didn't know anyone, and he soon found out that Verdance didn't have a YMCA or a homeless shelter where he could take refuge. That was puzzling.

At least the night wasn't too cold. He found a place in the park where he could shift into his poodle form—standard, not miniature—which was warmer, and he holed up in a thick stand of bushes. If anyone took a closer look, they wouldn't see anything. His curly black fur blended in with the darkness and shadows, and he was a large enough dog so most urban predators would steer clear.

Still, it was too cold to get comfortable, even when he curled up and pulled his backpack on top of him, and the ground was surprisingly rocklike. As exhausted as he was, it still took him a long time to fall asleep.

In the morning, he shifted back and hurriedly dressed. Even before dawn broke, people were out and about, and he startled a jogger as he emerged from his thicket. Every part of his body ached, and the chill left a lingering lethargy in his bones.

He bought a yogurt parfait and a coffee from a shop and hurried to the theater. When the doors opened at nine, he was the first one inside. He used the extra time to take an airport bath in the restroom before joining the others for stretching and warm-ups.

After a half hour to learn a short routine, the group took the stage. Each dancer wore a paper number. From the darkness of the seats, the director of choreography called out dismissals. "Thirteen—thank you. Two—thank you."

Never had a pleasantry carried such ominous intent. Marcel threw himself into the dance, channeling the mood of the music. Though he was feeling it, he kept his head in the game, careful to make sure his movements had elegance as well as attitude. He jumped a little higher than the dancers on either side of him, showing off his superior skills.

He was rewarded when the director of choreography said nothing at all to him until the performance ended. The DC came onstage for a closer look. He was a tall man with thick muscles and strong bone structure—the exact kind of build that made Marcel want to fan himself.

"My name is Germaine, which you have now earned the right to use. Rest up for a bit. Get some water, maybe an energy bar. You'll spend the afternoon learning a more complicated dance sequence, and I'll be making my final determinations from there."

The guy next to Marcel, a short man with straight blond hair and blue eyes, lifted a hand. "Germaine, when will we find out what part we got?"

Germaine responded with a scathing look. He flipped imaginary hair—his tight curls were buzzed short—and exited the stage. "Next group—you're up."

The guy opened his mouth to say more, but Marcel grabbed his arm. "The schedule is on the back of the lines we got yesterday. There's another callback tomorrow."

"Oh. Thanks." The guy rolled his eyes. "I should have looked." They entered the practice room, where the guy draped a towel around his neck and downed a bottle of water.

Marcel did the same. In the back of his mind, he realized he should economize, but a workout like that wrung him out. He wished he had a power bar, but he didn't. Glancing around, he wondered whether there might be a vending machine nearby.

"What are you looking for?" Blond guy asked. He looked like someone who'd been spoiled with endless dance lessons and whose parents had paid for him to tour with elite troupes.

"Vending machine."

The guy threw a power bar to Marcel. "I'm Holden. You're not from around here, are you?"

"Thanks." Marcel ripped open the wrapper and shook his head as he tore off a bite. "No. I'm in town for auditions. Are you from around here?"

Holden laughed. "Pleasance. It's the nearest major city, but it's lost even deeper in the mountains. Verdance has a theater, where Pleasance does not." He slung his bag over his shoulder and motioned to the door. "Come on."

"Where?"

"It's good to get out. I'll show you around."

They walked for a bit, and Holden showed him sights he'd already discovered, like the park and fountain, and he pointed out the best places to eat. Given the expensive look to the restaurants, they reinforced the image of a spoiled rich Marcel had formulated. Realizing that he was jealous—his parents had paid for one dance class per semester, not the five Marcel had wanted to take—Marcel concentrated on the positives. Holden seemed friendly, and he bought lunch for Marcel.

"Where are you staying?" Marcel wondered if Holden knew of cheaper accommodations.

"I have a friend who lives nearby. He's letting me sleep on his sofa for a couple nights. If I land this gig, I'm going to be part of the working poor." He laughed joyfully. "Verdance Theater has rooms you can let if you're in one of their plays. When it's busy, they stuff five or six people in a room the size of a shoebox, and rent is ten dollars a day."

"Wow. That sounds terrible." Marcel was used to sharing space with his siblings, but that was different. Strangers wouldn't all shift into canines and snuggle in a pile for warmth. "No privacy at all."

"Nope." Holden laughed again. "This sounds dumb, but I'm looking forward to it. It's like a rite of passage."

Though it didn't sound like a rite of passage Marcel wanted to experience in the least, a week later, he found himself on a bottom bunk in a room where three sets of narrow bunk beds took up all the available space. If they wanted to stand up, they had to climb out into the hallway. There was no way that setup didn't violate at least fifteen fire codes, but nobody was going to report it. There was no other housing to be had nearby. Holden was two rooms over, but the pair managed to develop a friendship. Neither had landed a speaking part. Marcel was simultaneously disappointed and elated, which was a curious combination of feelings.

He was elated to be part of the cast, but he was disappointed to have only landed a part as a dancer and choral singer.

Some days the constant social demands of his housing arrangement were too much, and so Marcel found himself drawn to the park. It had a different energy, and though there were people all around, the trees absorbed much of the noise, giving the place a relaxing vibe. The tinkling splash of water from the fountain had a soothing cadence, and he could lean back on a bench and snooze in relative peace.

On a Tuesday when he had the afternoon off, he found himself doing that exact thing. He set his backpack on the bench next to him. Because there was no real privacy where he was living, he kept his valuables with him—a small amount of cash, his identification, photos of his family, a novel he'd checked out of the library, and his favorite clothes. Big city dancers were vicious when it came to "borrowing" things from one another. Marcel was not willing to play those games.

He crossed his arms and rested his chin on his chest. In moments, he was asleep. He started awake sometime later with the feeling that something wasn't right. His backpack, which had been half on his lap, was gone.

Jumping to his feet, he was on high alert. He scanned the scattered crowd for someone carrying his backpack. Across the park, he spotted a dark-haired man scurrying out the far gate.

With a sudden bark—such things sometimes couldn't be helped— he raced around the fountain, shouting for the thief to stop. Around him, people's activities paused as he ran past them. They lifted their faces and looked.

Marcel was fast. He imagined himself a handsome blur in the eyes of the human observers. The thief seemed unaware he was in Marcel's crosshairs. Marcel leaped the last few feet, tackling the bandit to the ground.

Well, that's the way it should have happened. Instead, Marcel ended up with his arms around the man's neck and his legs wrapped around the man's waist. Given the distance and Marcel's agitation, he hadn't realized the large stature of the thief.

The man twisted around, trying to dislodge Marcel. "What are you doing?" He growled, his whole chest vibrating with brutal intensity.

"That's my backpack. You stole my backpack!" Marcel shouted, hoping to attract the attention of the authorities.

The man pried loose from Marcel's hold and dropped him to the ground like a rancid sack of potatoes. He gazed down at Marcel, eyes narrowed to make his sharp features even more pointed. "That's absurd. This is my bag."

"It's not! It's mine. It was on my lap, you snake!"

The man heaved a sigh and regarded Marcel as if he was an annoying child. "We're finished here."

He turned away, and red clouds of fury clouded Marcel's brain. He ran at the robber, hitting him low enough to take him down. The pair tumbled onto the asphalt. In a shocking display of strength, the thief threw Marcel from his body and into the street. He hit the cement hard, bouncing on the unforgiving surface as white-hot pain streaked through his arm, tailbone, and ankle. Brakes screeched, and Marcel's life flashed before his eyes.

Moments later, hands were on his body. He opened his eyes and tried to sit up, but agony wouldn't let him move. The woman hovering over him made a disapproving noise, and her gentle touch pinned his shoulder down. "Stay put. The ambulance is on its way."

"My backpack," Marcel rasped. "He stole my backpack."

Chapter 2

"I don't understand why I'm here." Amaricio Granger folded his hands over his flat stomach and pouted, if a six-and-a-half-foot tall alpha dragon shifter with an imposing and often ominous bearing could be described as pouting.

As Head of Security for Draco International, Ezekiel Lowry knew why each person in the room was present. They were there because they had intimate knowledge of the project Tito Kaysar obsessed over, and they knew the nefarious lengths through which he would and had gone to make progress on said project. Almost a year ago, Kaysar had kidnapped Amar's pregnant omega to perform experiments on him. Edgar was a rarity these days—an omega who actually conceived offspring with a dragon shifter.

The fact that Edgar was a canine shifter bothered Kaysar—and a lot of other dragons—and so there had been no penalty for Tito's actions because the High Council of Dragon Elders cared only about dragonkind. Edgar was collateral damage.

When the High Council released Tito, they'd tasked him with continuing his experiments. The only difference lay in the fact that he was required to get permission from the subject of the test before conducting any experiments.

Tito had immediately thrust the task upon Koren Tafari, the brilliant scientist in charge of R&D. Koren himself had recently mated with a canine shifter, and the pair was now married. Koren's omega, Chayton, had given birth to a litter of two a little over six months ago.

"I want an update," Tito explained. "Koren?"

Amar got to his feet. "I'm not staying for this."

"You'll sit down," Tito ordered. As he was the CEO of Draco International, a leader in the Sharp-Winged Tribe, and he'd mentored each of the men in the room, his word was law.

Amar didn't bother to disguise his hatred for Tito or his disgust for the project as he resumed his seat.

Koren, who hadn't been happy about the assignment, shuffled through a folder full of papers he'd brought. Despite his initial distaste for the project, Koren's scientific curiosity and common sense had helped him see the merit in the study. Though their friendship was solid, Amar had warned Koren neither he nor his family would participate in the research.

In a brilliant, but evil, move, Tito had put Koren in charge of the project, not only because he was the smartest person any of them knew, but because he thought Koren might be able to convince Amar to change his mind.

Instead, Koren had consented to using his omega and his children for the study. He came to the page he'd been looking for. "I'm finished sequencing all the DNA."

"That took a lot longer than I expected," Tito noted.

Koren pressed his lips together. He also resented Tito's return. "I'm not a geneticist. I had to learn how to use all the equipment, and sequencing the unknown takes longer than sequencing something already widely available to the scientific community."

"Plus he had to learn genetics," Eli added. As VP of Marketing, Eli Dionicio held an ambiguous position in the company that allowed him to monitor public perception of dragons and keep ahead of anyone or anything that might threaten to expose them to the world. In the digital age, this had become an increasingly difficult job, and Eli had become a master of disinformation.

He was a good friend, someone who'd always looked out for Zeke.

"Not many people can learn an entirely new field of study in six months." Zeke spoke up to defend Koren as well because he knew Amar would not. He was still too angry about what happened to Edgar to care about the bigger picture.

Koren wasn't jazzed about it either, but he wanted to know if there would be problems down the road for his children. As a general rule, shifters of all breeds didn't shift until puberty, and so they had no clues as to how the children would develop or what they'd shift into.

Tito wasn't a stupid man. Nobody rose to his level of power and prestige without understanding how to read a room. He knew none of them trusted him in the least, just as he knew they wouldn't suddenly stage a coup. If they did, the High Council would gather troops to assassinate every last one of the insurgents. If they were going to win this, they had to play Kaysar's game.

Ignoring everything else, he gestured toward Koren. "Tafari, continue."

"The sequencing is complete. I'm in the process of comparing parent and offspring DNA to identify differences."

Amar's scowl darkened his already swarthy face. "You're talking about your omega and your sons as if they're not people, as if they mean nothing to you."

"They mean everything to me," Koren returned quietly. "Which is why I'm doing this."

This was an old argument. Koren maintained knowledge was power, and Amar didn't want that kind of power anywhere near Kaysar.

Zeke didn't know what Koren was holding back from Kaysar, but he knew his friend wasn't about to spill his guts. The knowledge he shared would be strategic, and whatever he kept back would be enough to keep Kaysar from gaining more power.

Rather than debate with Amar, Koren continued the debrief. "It would be helpful if I had a larger sample size. Anshu Bray of the Ice-Breather Tribe has sequenced DNA from dozens of shifter species. I'd like access to his data."

Tito considered this carefully. "I'm not sure I can get what you need. Granger torched that bridge pretty thoroughly when he rejected Anshu as a mate. Even if I could get my counterpart at Gliding Principles to agree, I'm not sure Bray wouldn't destroy the information rather than hand it over."

Koren cleared his throat. "There is a way of appealing to Anshu directly."

Dread tickled Zeke's protective instincts, the same ones that had helped him rise to Head of Security in ten short years. He devoted the entirety of his attention to Koren.

"He wants an alpha. I'm not sure if he's looking to get married or just get laid, but Anshu Bray, the only dragon omega we know about, is a virgin. None of the alphas in the Ice-Breather Tribe have shown an interest in him." Koren followed up with an ironic, dry chuckle.

Zeke stared. "Are you saying you want me to procure a sexual partner for him in order to persuade him to share years of meticulous research?"

Koren lifted a shoulder. "It's an idea."

"Wait," Amar said. "Are you saying Bray isn't in high demand among the Ice-Breathers? That's insane. They have the only dragon omega in the world. You'd think they'd be lining up and begging for a chance to be his mate."

"You didn't," Eli pointed out. "He went all the way to South America to marry you, without having met you, and you rejected him outright."

"I had an omega," Amar growled. "There are plenty of unattached alphas available."

"Yes," Kaysar interrupted. "At the time, I was unaware of your liaison, otherwise I might have chosen Eli or Ezekiel."

"Why not you?" Zeke challenged Kaysar. "You're unattached. Come to think of it, I've never seen you with anyone, not even for a casual date."

14

Tito pressed his lips together, and his expression closed off. He wasn't going to answer.

"Are you too good for the last omega on Earth?" Zeke pressed. "If he's so valuable a commodity, why don't *you* want him? Think of the power and prestige that would come from possibly siring other omegas."

"He's heterosexual." Though it was a guess—because none of them had proof—Koren spoke with quiet authority. "He doesn't find men attractive. He likes the ladies."

"Huh," Eli said. "That explains a lot."

Amar's eyes glittered with amusement, but he said nothing.

Shifters, as a rule, were homosexual. Men mated with men, and women mated with women. That was the natural order of things. Few were bisexual, and even fewer were heterosexual. It was a curious development.

"Holy shit." Koren's eyes widened. "I just realized I have seen you on dates. When I've seen you out with a woman, I've always assumed they were friends—but they weren't, were they? And there was that one you went out with for two years."

Understanding that cornering Tito wasn't a good idea, Zeke tried to resume control of the conversation. "Tito, it's okay, you know. It's modern times. You don't have to live in the closet anymore. You can be open about your sexuality. We won't judge you on that."

"Yeah." Amar's deep voice amplified Zeke's assurance. "There are so many other things to judge you about."

At that moment, Zeke's work cell buzzed. Though he had no intention of answering, he liked to know who made demands on his time. The display showed Armon from HR. He let it go to voicemail.

Immediately, it buzzed again, this time with a text. *Call immed. Emergency. Need you.*

Zeke got up and went to a corner of the room to return the call. "Armon, what's going on?"

Armon's explanation came in a breathy rush. "Zane Velan called. I looked him up, but he doesn't work for DI. He said to tell you that he was in jail in Verdance, and someone needs to bail him out. I wasn't going to interrupt your meeting, but then someone named Antares called. He said that he was Mr. Kaysar's boss, and I was to immediately take care of Mr. Velan's situation. I don't know who these people are, but I didn't want to lose my job. So I called security, and they said I had to talk to you."

Bailing random people out of jail wasn't in Zeke's official job description, but as Head of Security, he was somewhat of a fixer for the

Sharp-Winged Tribe. Zane Velan was the attorney who'd presented the case for keeping Tito Kaysar behind bars. Officially he worked for the High Council, and all Sharp-Winged dragons answered to their governing body.

He had no choice but to post bail for the attorney. "I'll take care of it, Armon. Thanks for letting me know."

The noise level of the conversation in the room was rising. Zeke rushed to handle the situation at hand.

Koren slammed his folder shut. "You date shifters from other species and even humans, and you have the nerve to pretend outrage because Amar and I fell for canine shifters? That's just wrong."

"Yep." Amar's eyes sparkled with irony and malice. "We can judge you for that too."

This was spiraling out of control. His friends had been waiting for a moment of vulnerability to pounce on Tito.

"Enough," Zeke decreed. "Let's get back to the matter at hand. Tito, begin negotiations with Gliding Principles for access. Eli and Amar, start making a list of every unmated alpha we know, and then dig deeper for ones from other tribes, maybe the Fire-Breathers or the Silver-Winged. Get it to me ASAP."

Tito lifted a brow, probably at the idea Zeke—or any underling—would assign him a task.

"Just do it," Zeke said. "Or rescind your order for Koren to complete this project."

Amar sat up straighter, and Koren's gaze dropped.

"No," Tito said. "We'll follow your plan." He nodded to the group. "You have your assignments."

After he left, Zeke gathered his things.

"Where are you off to?" Eli asked.

"Jail." He didn't mince words, but he glanced at Koren. "Zane Velan has been arrested, and he's sitting inside lockup right now. Want to come with me?"

Zeke and Koren had gone to the trial to testify against Tito. Amar had been too emotionally involved, and so the High Council hadn't wanted him as a witness, and Eli didn't have more to add than Zeke or Koren. Therefore, Koren was the only other person in the room who'd met Zane.

"Who is Zane Velan?" Eli asked.

"Lawyer who argued against Tito being released." Koren scooped up his folder. "I promised Chay I'd be home at a reasonable time, otherwise I'd go."

"I'll go," Amar volunteered. "I'd like to meet him. Edgar will understand." He moved off to the other end of the room with his cell phone to inform his omega of the change in plans. Since dragons had excellent hearing, the distance afforded no additional privacy if anyone in the room wished to listen in. Respect for Amaricio was the only reason nobody went out of their way to overhear.

At the police station, they were greeted by the Sergeant in charge. Marcie Mavensburg had been a mainstay at Verdance PD for forty years, and she knew why the executives from Draco International looked like they hadn't aged a day. Though she was human, she was someone Zeke trusted. Her family had descended from the original settlers, a people who had originally been a servant class to the ruling dragons.

Marcie's hair should have been gray, but she was dedicated to being a redhead, so that was the color she stuck by. She came out from behind the safety glass and hugged him. "Zeke Lowry, to what do I owe this honor?"

He returned the hug, and kissed the top of her head. "A friend of ours was picked up earlier today, and I came down to see if I couldn't straighten things out."

"Sure. Who is it?" Her eyes widened, and she threw out a guess. "Zane Velan?"

"The same."

"He stole a backpack from a man, and then he assaulted the guy, throwing him into the street. He's lucky the driver of the truck barreling down the road saw the human missile in time to stop, otherwise he'd be facing a murder-two charge." Marcie sighed, her ample body heaving with the effort. "He's from Chile, which makes him a flight risk. I don't see the judge setting bail."

While Zeke tried to sort out the heap of information dumped on him, Amar stepped forward. "Hi, Marcie. It's been a while, so you might not remember me, but I'm Amaricio Granger."

"I remember you." She winked and pinched his cheek. "The shy one."

Zeke snorted at that. His friend might be reserved, but he was far from shy. "I don't understand, Marcie. There has to be more to the story. Zane isn't the kind of man who would do those things. Perhaps this man attacked Zane first, and he was just defending himself?"

Marcie shrugged. "I don't know anything more."

"Witness statements?" Zeke pressed.

"You're not a lawyer." She admonished him for crossing a line.

"No, but the more I know, the easier it will be for me to solve the problem."

This time, she snorted. "I know how you operate, Mr. Lowry. This man was minding his own business, napping on a bench after having lunch, when his backpack was stolen. He went after Mr. Velan, who still had the backpack, and he tried to take it back. I'm sure if he'd known why Mr. Velan is such a big fellow, he might have thought twice about acting alone."

Zeke couldn't wrap his head around the mild-mannered lawyer having done any of those things.

"That's according to witness statements?" Amar asked. "What did you say the victim's name was?"

Marcie shook her finger at Amar. "It's the quiet ones you have to watch yourself around. You're not going to charm me into revealing the victim's name or whereabouts, mister."

"The hospital," Zeke guessed. "You said he was messed up."

"Don't you even think of threatening that poor young man." She switched her finger-shaking to Zeke. "He's been through enough."

Zeke held up his hands. "Marcie, I swear I have good intentions."

She stopped with the finger, and she retreated behind the bulletproof glass window. "I know you—you're going to offer to pay that man's medical bills. That's an admission of guilt, which means you'll assume civil liability. Your generosity is going to end up costing you big time."

He held his hand over his heart and slid a flirty smile onto his face. "Marcie, you're much too sweet for this job. Come work for me. I'll set you up with a comfortable office and underlings to order around."

She chuckled. "I have that now." Then she sobered. "Seriously— Draco International employs half the people in this town, either directly or indirectly. We can't have you drained into bankruptcy."

Amar leaned closer to the small hole in the glass. "Rest assured that we are solvent, and we're insured against lawsuits, civil or otherwise."

Marcie shook her head, and then she buzzed them into the office proper. It was full of cubicles, though many were empty because they were out on patrol or calls. She led them to a cubicle in the far corner. "Wait here, and I'll see if I can track down the arresting officer."

While she was gone, Zeke settled on the business side of the desk and opened up recent incident reports. "Marcel Yardan, taken to Verdance Community Hospital. They haven't questioned him yet."

"What's the plan?" Amar asked.

"You wait here and press for a bail hearing today. I'll go see Mr. Yardan, see if I can't get him to drop the charges." He slapped Amar's shoulder. "Thanks for coming. You're a real help."

A half hour later, Zeke signed into the hospital as a visitor, and he found Mr. Yardan's room without incident. He'd been admitted to a short-term observation unit, which meant they weren't sure as to the extent of his injuries. After a brief knock on the open door, he entered the room. Seeing the man propped up against the raised back of the bed sent a shockwave through Zeke's body.

It wasn't the large bandages that covered the side of his head and his exposed shoulder or the splint on his arm that caused any kind of reaction. Zeke had been through enough battles to have seen every kind of wound imaginable, as well as a few that were difficult to conceive. No, this was a shock of awareness on the part of his dragon, and he'd never before felt anything like it.

Caught by surprise at this new, surreal feeling, Zeke found himself momentarily dumbstruck. His dragon came to the fore, exercising dominion by sharpening his senses. He noted the damages, sensing the concussion, broken bones, multiple contusions, and the tender ankle. Simultaneously he took in the long, sinewy muscles the shapeless hospital gown and the blanket draped over his legs couldn't quite camouflage.

He had a powerful urge to taste Marcel Yardan. He wanted to know the exact flavor of his kiss, his dark chocolate skin, and his seed. His dragon purred insistently, demanding a sample, and Zeke had every intention of indulging it.

"You're not the doctor."

The voice jerked Zeke from the primal reverie that had overtaken him. He glanced to his left to find a man seated in a chair next to the bed. With his highlighted blond hair and cornflower blue eyes to bring out his handsomeness, and a ripped body to match, this man qualified as a potential impediment to Zeke's claiming of his mate.

That man had noted his non-medical status.

Zeke drew himself up, puffing out his chest to appear even larger. "You're not the patient."

The guy's gaze wandered Zeke's body. "You're not a relative, either."

Gritting his teeth, Zeke threw the observation back. "Nor are you."

"Friend," the blond said. He looked to Marcel. "You know this guy?"

Marcel seemed dazed. He stared at Zeke. After a long time, a response croaked from his throat. "No."

Zeke reached toward the tray next to the bed. "You need water." He held the cup to Marcel's lips while the potential omega sipped.

After a bit, Marcel leaned back. "Thank you. I didn't catch your name or why you're here."

"Ezekiel Lowry, but my friends call me Zeke."

Marcel offered his hand. "I'm Marcel, and this is my friend, Holden."

The first contact of skin sent a jolt of electricity and need through Zeke, and it left Marcel with a more confused wrinkle to his lovely chin. "I'm the Head of Security for Draco International."

"Oh," Holden gasped. "You're from the theater?"

A bit of Marcel's confusion leaped to Zeke. "Theater?"

Holden sat up straighter and clasped his hands in front of his chest. "The Verdance Theater. Draco International is a major sponsor of the arts. They have the biggest banners in the lobby."

Zeke shrugged. Amar would know more about where DI spent their money. "I'm in security, not philanthropy."

"Mr. Lowry, why are you here?" Marcel asked.

It bothered Zeke that Marcel didn't treat him with familiarity. He didn't want any barriers of propriety standing between them. He considered Holden, and all the ways in which he was an impediment. "Holden, can you step out into the hall and give us a moment?"

Holden, to his credit, looked to Marcel to see what he wanted.

Marcel pressed his luscious lips together, no doubt waging an internal struggle between unexplained urges and his better sense. Zeke recognized this because he was also navigating those turbulent waters.

Finally, he shook his head, a tiny movement that ran counter to what his animal wanted. Zeke assumed Marcel was a shifter because, otherwise, why would his dragon be so insistent? Marcel ran his tongue along his luscious lower lip. "Holden stays."

Zeke motioned to an unoccupied chair. "Mind if I sit?"

"Knock yourself out." Marcel watched, half wary and half curious, as Zeke slid a heavy chair closer and sat down.

"I'm here to negotiate a settlement. In return for dropping the charges against Zane Velan, we're willing to pay all medical costs associated with the accident."

Marcel's lower lip stuck out, and Zeke's dragon surged to the fore, insisting on a nibble. He breathed to control his reaction, and a bit of steam came out of his nose. He hoped nobody noticed.

Rescinding the subconscious invitation, Marcel scowled and scoffed. "It wasn't an accident. He stole everything I own, and then he threw me in front of a moving vehicle."

Marcie had indicated as much, but Zeke had faith that Zane had a good explanation. He needed Amar to post bail so that he could hear it.

Without Zane's account, Zeke was flying blind. "You're sure it was *your* backpack?"

Marcel narrowed his eyes.

"Yes," Holden said. "He's sure, and so are the po-po. They're holding it as evidence. They have everything Marcel brought to Verdance with him, including clothes, ID, and money."

Zeke seized upon that admission. "If you drop the charges, you'll get back all your stuff."

"Don't do it," Holden said. "You can't dance on that ankle, which means you're going to lose your spot, and if you're not working for the Verdance Theater, they're going to kick you out of your room."

So, the omega his dragon wanted was soon to be jobless and homeless due to this attack. It was a horrible position for negotiation for Marcel, but it was wonderful for Zeke. He chose to use it as incentive. "Marcel, let us pay your medical costs as well as punitive damages. We'll pay your housing costs for three months, and give you a monthly stipend for food and incidentals. A sprained ankle and broken arm will heal by then."

It would also give Zeke enough time to win Marcel's heart and establish his place as Zeke's omega. Marcel would never want for anything again.

Marcel didn't seem pleased by the offer. He attempted to cross his arms, but grimaced at the movement. Zeke was on his feet, his hands gentle as he helped reposition Marcel's wounded arm.

"Be careful, Marcel." The name rolled from his tongue, a verbal caress that washed through his heart and gathered a hint of reverence. "They haven't set the bone. I'll get them on that as soon as possible. You shouldn't be forced to wait on proper care."

In his brief ministration, he managed to brush his fingertips across the exposed skin on Marcel's arm. It calmed his dragon while also making him yearn for more than incidental contact.

Marcel studied the ceiling. "All medical bills, no exceptions, for a year. An apartment with at least three rooms for a year. A thousand dollars a month for a year."

Zeke would have given him a lot more if he'd asked. A thousand dollars a month wasn't much when it came to food costs. Dragons had hearty appetites, and Zeke spent significantly more than that on groceries every month. Well, it was obvious Marcel wasn't a dragon. Given what had happened to two of Zeke's friends, it stood to reason that Marcel was probably a canine shifter. Koren was going to have more fodder for his research very soon.

Still, this was a negotiation, and he was compelled to offer less. Once Zeke had claimed Marcel, none of this would matter anyway. He would see to his omega's every need. "All related medical bills, including follow-up care, for a year. An apartment for six months. We can agree to a thousand-dollar stipend each month, but you'll have to agree to a regular review of your case."

Yeah, he was negotiating for dates. "Regular" could mean anything from daily to weekly to monthly, provided the interval remained the same.

"Regular? Like weekly?"

Zeke shrugged. "More often at first. Less often as you heal."

Holden snorted. Zeke had forgotten the man was there. Who was he, exactly? A friend, he could handle. But given how physically pleasing his features were, it was likely that Holden and Marcel were romantically involved. That would need to stop now.

As a way to rein in his jealousy, Zeke concentrated on the screen monitoring Marcel's vitals. He couldn't go around issuing dictates to the omega—yet. Marcel had already proven himself intelligent and headstrong. While Zeke prized those qualities, it meant he would need to work harder to winnow his way into Marcel's heart.

"The apartment needs to be downtown, near the theater," Holden added.

Zeke studied both men. "You're actors?"

"Featured dancers," Holden corrected. "We both have solos in *Dance of the Dragons.*"

Zeke had never heard of it, but that wasn't surprising. He couldn't recall the last time he'd gone to the theater. Tito liked to go, and Amar went regularly because Edgar enjoyed it. He'd poked fun at Amar for purchasing season tickets for his omega, and now it looked like karma had taken a huge chunk out of Zeke's hide.

With a sprained ankle, Marcel would likely lose his job as a dancer because he was easily replaceable. Zeke might need to pull strings to help his intended omega land a part in another production.

He got to his feet. "I'll return with paperwork, and you'll need to formally withdraw your complaint to halt charges against Mr. Velan."

On the way out, he phoned DI's lawyers, and by the time he made it to the office, they had the contract ready. Additionally they'd dispatched a representative to the police station to help secure Zane Velan's freedom.

As much as Zeke knew he needed to hear Velan's side of the story, he followed his instinct to return to the hospital with two lawyers, and he was happy to see Holden had left. He hovered in the background while they presented the contract to Marcel.

Maeve Gilly flashed a sympathetic smile at Marcel. "Mr. Yardan, this is a standard settlement by which we admit no wrongdoing, and you are prohibited from disclosing the terms to anyone."

Marcel's gaze zeroed on Zeke. "He knows, as does my friend Holden. You're going to have to take out the gag order."

Eithann, the second lawyer, swooped in. "It's a standard part of the contract. It can't be removed."

Marcel's smile exactly mirrored Maeve's. "Nice try. I come from a family of lawyers. If you don't want me to bring in my own people and have you pay for their services, then take out the clause."

When Eithann and Maeve opened their mouths to refuse, Marcel laughed. "Come on. I'm not after money, otherwise I would have gone to law school like my parents wanted. However, I know that if I were to press charges and then sue you for damages, I'd be walking away with millions. Take out the clause."

At that moment, Zeke understood Marcel wasn't motivated by money or material goods. He had dreams, and he was intent on achieving them. Zeke clamped a hand on Eithann's shoulder. "Remove the clause."

Though the expression on his face indicated a severe reluctance, he didn't argue with Zeke. He opened up the contract and crossed out the offending section. "The rest lists the benefits. Draco International will assume payment for all medical costs associated with documented injuries from the incident. Additionally, DI will pay rent and utilities for six months on an apartment and issue Mr. Yardan a stipend of two thousand dollars per month for six months."

Marcel frowned. "We agreed on one thousand, not two."

Maeve glared. "You're going to argue with more money?"

"Well, it wasn't the deal we made."

"Take it," Zeke counseled. "Living in Verdance is more expensive than you seem to think."

Placing the palm of his good hand against his forehead, Marcel groaned. "I hadn't thought about furnishing it."

"It's a corporate apartment," Zeke said. "It's furnished."

"Yes," Maeve confirmed. "When you vacate the apartment, the furniture stays. It is the property of Draco International."

"Sure." Marcel held out his good hand. "I want to read the contract."

Eithann handed it over. The trio waited in silence while Marcel read. The lawyers seemed to anticipate questions, while Zeke was content to watch over the omega.

He wanted everyone to be gone so he could act on his instinct. His dragon purred now, but it also thundered for possession of the omega. It was becoming more and more difficult to control, and the longer he denied it, the harder it fought for release.

Chapter 3

Marcel

Eventually the contract was signed, and the lawyers left.

Mr. Lowry stood at the foot of Marcel's bed, openly studying him in a way that made Marcel struggle not to squirm. He felt like prey. The man was impossibly big, with broad shoulders that spanned almost the width of Marcel's bed. He seemed extra tall. Holden had estimated the security man's height at close to seven feet, and Marcel was inclined to agree. The man was endowed with massive, thick muscles that the elegant cut of his suit couldn't quite hide. He was a handsome devil with close-shaved brown hair and sparkling blue eyes. If Mr. Lowry tried out for a play, he'd beat out everyone for the lead. The man had presence and an attitude that assured he always achieved his goals.

His expression seemed neutral, though his eyes betrayed his attraction to Marcel. After several silent moments, his lips parted. "You're a shifter, but I can't figure out what kind."

The question did not shock Marcel. He'd suspected that Mr. Lowry was a shifter, a large one, based on his massive size in human form. Though shifters didn't go around outing themselves, it was generally considered safe to disclose his identity to another shifter. Marcel grinned. "I thought I felt a connection to you. That explains it. I'm a poodle. What are you?"

The smoking hot Mr. Lowry didn't alter his expression. "Dragon."

Immediately, Marcel laughed at the deadpan delivery. He loved a man with a sense of humor. Lifting his good hand, he excused Mr. Lowry's evasion. "Okay, don't tell me, though I'm not sure why you think you need to keep it a secret."

Now the shifter had an expression. His eyes widened with shock, and his jaw dropped open. "I am a dragon. Verdance is home base to the Sharp-Winged Tribe. We run Draco International."

Dragons were mythical creatures, and Marcel was no fool. He spread his palm wide. "Show me."

That startled expression added an element of disbelief. "No."

He let his hand drop to his thigh. "You're allowed to have secrets. After all, we're not friends, and we're not likely to become friends."

Mr. Lowry gripped Marcel's footboard. "Why not?"

"I think it's obvious." This time, Marcel's laugh betrayed a hint of nerves. He couldn't figure out why his emotions were so volatile, but then he figured it had to do with shock.

Rather than admit Marcel was right, Mr. Lowry lifted his sculpted brows. No man had a right to look that good without lots of hours of prep. "Enlighten me."

"You're protecting the man who hurt me. It's the sort of conflict of interest that precludes friendship."

The big man's hold eased, and when he let go of the metal and plastic footboard, Marcel noted that he'd left fingerprint dents in the molded material. He closed the door and perched on the edge of Marcel's bed. Taking Marcel's good hand between his, he said, "I disagree."

Suddenly Marcel's chest felt tight, and he had trouble getting the words out. The skin-to-skin contact was frying his brain, and his inner dog whined to get closer. It took everything he had to refrain from sliding onto Mr. Lowry's lap. His voice shook when he replied. "That's your right."

"One might argue I've protected *you*. With the resources of DI at his disposal, Velan could have delayed a criminal proceeding for months, and a civil one indefinitely. You need housing and funds now."

Marcel realized one universal truth at that moment. "You did it because you want to have sex with me."

"While that may be true, it's not the main reason."

Glad that Mr. Lowry didn't try to deny what was right there in both their faces, Marcel tugged his hand from the alpha's grasp. He needed to get his dog under control. "What is the main reason?"

Mr. Lowry stood, and Marcel felt the loss as a resounding ache. The larger man paced to the window and pushed aside the thick curtain. Rays of late afternoon sunlight lit shafts of dust in the room.

Marcel let his gaze outline the way the larger shifter's sexy legs led to a delightfully rounded ass, though most of that was a guess because Mr. Lowry still wore his suit jacket. "Mr. Lowry?"

"Zeke." He said his name like an order, and Marcel wondered whether he should follow the directive.

On one hand, it implied a level of familiarity that wasn't true. On the other hand, it could lead to the kind of friendship that included acting on their baser desires. He was against starting something physical with this alpha because it would interfere with his plans to be a star on the stage.

Mr. Lowry dropped the curtain and turned back to face Marcel. "Marcel, say my name."

Making a choice that caused his heart to stutter erratically, Marcel said, "Mr. Lowry."

His face darkened. Ruddy with contained fury, he clenched his fists. "Omega, I have limits, and you are fast approaching them."

Marcel wasn't from a submissive line of omegas. "Well, your inability to answer simple questions is kind of pissing me off as well, so why don't you leave now?"

The glower should have struck fear into Marcel's heart, but it only made him bolder and more reckless. He arched a single brow, daring Mr. Lowry to press the point. When the alpha's gaze slid away, Marcel celebrated internally with an imagined victory dance.

When his gaze once again focused on Marcel, he made it clear Marcel was mistaken. Mr. Lowry was allowing him room to not lose face, but he wasn't ceding the point. "We will resume this discussion when your injuries have had a chance to mend. I'll see that your arm is set now."

Marcel was amazed at how quickly Mr. Lowry got things done. People scurried to do his bidding, though they seemed more respectful than afraid. Within fifteen minutes, a specialist was in his room, pointing out things on an x-ray.

"It's a hairline fracture, so you won't need surgery to set it." The middle-aged man with salt-and-pepper hair and a white lab coat unwrapped the bandage on his arm. "We'll need to wait for the swelling to go down a bit more. I'm going to keep you on the anti-inflammatory, and I'll check back in the morning. Do you have any questions?"

"Will this limit my movement or how much I can lift? I'm a dancer, and I do gymnastics in a lot of my routines. Sometimes I lift people." Unless a woman was involved, Marcel was usually the one lifted, as he was a bit on the petite side.

"You should be back to your regular activities in about twelve or sixteen weeks. It's a fracture, so you won't have to worry about it limiting your activity once it's healed." He gestured to Marcel's ankle. "That's going to take longer to heal and come back than your arm will. Once it's better, you'll need to see a sports medicine specialist. I have a colleague who deals mostly with dancers and gymnasts. I'll write a referral."

When the doctor left, Mr. Lowry came back into his room. "What did Dr. Minetta say?"

Ah, that was the specialist's name. Marcel grinned. "Don't you know?"

"No." Mr. Lowry scowled. "HIPPA laws won't let your doctor tell me anything without your permission."

"But you're paying the bills." Marcel enjoyed having the upper hand for now, so he withheld the information.

Mr. Lowry's expression didn't soften. "Itemized bills will go through DI's lawyers for vetting, but they're still confidential."

"Oh." A wave of exhaustion swept over Marcel, and he relented. "He wants to wait another day for the swelling to go down before he puts a cast on it. He said my ankle is going to need physical therapy to get it back into shape for dancing."

A knock sounded on the door. Mr. Lowry answered it. "Amar, thanks for bringing this. I'll just be a moment." He reached to where Marcel couldn't see, and when his arm came back, he was holding Marcel's backpack. "Where do you want this?"

Marcel held out his good hand. The moment Mr. Lowry set it down next to him, he checked the contents. Someone had gone through it because nothing was how he'd packed it. Nevertheless, he identified his clothes, ID, cell phone, and money. His cell had a million messages. Finding everything there, he closed his eyes in relief. "Thank you for this."

Without asking, Mr. Lowry took Marcel's cell phone and tapped at the screen. "I'm adding my number to your contacts list. Call if you need anything." And then he was gone.

Marcel felt the emptiness immediately. In a short time, he'd become used to the alpha's presence, and he liked the big man's attention. He looked at the new contact to find that Mr. Lowry had programmed his name in as simply Zeke—no last name. It was a pointed message that made Marcel kind of excited to see how far he could push the handsome alpha before he lost his temper.

Closing his eyes, he pushed away the intense attraction he felt for the supposed dragon shifter, and he called his fathers. He took pride in the fact he wasn't going to need them to come rescue him from his mistakes. Yes, he was bound to lose his position in *Dance of the Dragons*, but due to the deal he'd struck, now he had time to heal and to try again. All was not lost.

And yet, he still felt the bitterness and resentfulness that came with losing out on his initial chance to perform on stage.

Zeke

Exiting the room, Zeke found Amar leaning against the wall across the hall, his attention on his phone.

"Sexting the mister?"

Amar glanced up. "Huh? No, Edgar sent a video of the triplets hugging each other. It's damn cute, but it looks more like wrestling."

Zeke held out his hand. "Aww. Can I see?"

Though he handed over his phone, Amar eyed Zeke curiously. "You're not really someone who is amused by the antics of children."

Until today, the offspring of his friends had been creatures he was sworn to protect. Now he felt more of a connection, and while he silently fawned over the adorable one-year-olds engaged in hugs that knocked down their sibling, outwardly he gave Amar back his phone. "You were right."

It wasn't until they were alone in the car that Amar brought it up again. "Zeke, are you feeling okay?"

"Yeah." He chose to deflect. "I wish I knew what went on from Velan's perspective. He's not the kind of person who steals things or attacks smaller shifters."

Amar perked up. "He's a shifter?"

"Yes."

"A dog shifter?"

"A poodle."

A slow grin spread across Amar's face. "Your dragon purred, didn't it?"

"It did," Zeke begrudgingly admitted. "But I still negotiated the settlement down to the bare minimum. He could have asked for a lot more. I was authorized to go as high as two million. All told, we're in this for less than a fifty thousand."

"As the person in charge of the finances, I thank you. If Zane hadn't fucked up, we wouldn't have spent anything." Amar drummed his fingers on his thigh. "But then you wouldn't have met your omega. Is he a regular-sized poodle or one of those toy-sized breeds?"

Not having seen Marcel shift, Zeke wasn't sure. He'd always fancied himself the kind of tough guy with a large breed dog, but it turned out not to matter what Marcel shifted into. He'd take him no matter what. "I don't know much about him. He's a dancer at the Verdance Theater, and he won't call me by my first name."

"Hmmm." Amar tapped his fingers a few more times. "Maybe he sees you as the enemy."

"The enemy? I tried to be upfront with him."

29

"You offered him money not to press charges against a man who attacked him, and then you told him he was destined to be your omega?" Somehow, Amar managed to deliver that question without an ironic edge to his tone.

"I didn't tell him much of anything." Zeke wiped his hand across his eyes and squeezed the bridge of his nose. "I'm not used to having to try. Men usually throw themselves at my feet. Marcel is unimpressed."

"You should ask Edgar," Amar said. "He's great at relationships. He helped Koren get things started with Chay."

Zeke didn't want to travel the route of gossip and advice. He wanted Marcel on his terms. "I have a few missiles in my arsenal yet."

"Suit yourself." A soft chuckle issued from Amar. "Just be warned that it's not going to stop Edgar from offering advice, and he's going to want to hear every last detail."

Rather than inform his friend that his omega was destined for disappointment, Zeke grunted. He dropped Amar at the door to his building. "I'll see you in the morning."

His next order of business was to visit Zane Velan, who was staying in a suite DI kept at a local hotel. Zeke rode the elevator to the ninth floor and knocked on the door.

It opened to reveal the top-level lawyer who worked for the High Council. Young and handsome, Zane was around a century old. His swarthy skin glowed with yellowish undertones. The sharp cheekbones and dark hair emphasized the light in his dark brown eyes. Though he was devastatingly handsome, Zane Velan had earned his spot and his reputation through intelligence, savvy decision-making, and grit. He flashed a brief smile. "I was hoping to surprise you."

The admission caught Zeke by surprise. He laughed. "Mission accomplished. I did not expect my day to unfold as it has."

Finding one's mate when omegas were scarce was always unexpected, and finding that one's mate wasn't eager or amenable was even more shocking. Instinct typically trumped everything else for a shifter.

Zane stepped back and spread his hand. "Come in. Have you had dinner yet? I was about to order room service."

Zeke had not eaten. "How about I treat you to a meal at my favorite steakhouse? You can tell me why you stole some random guy's backpack, and I can thank you for helping me find my omega."

In the midst of putting on his shoes, Zane stopped and looked up, both brows arching high. "The guy I inadvertently almost killed is your omega?"

"It seems so."

Zane finished his task and grabbed his jacket. "Amaricio said the young man will make a full recovery."

"He should. DI will pay for his care and physical therapy. He's a dancer, so he'll need a specialist for his ankle injury." Zeke motioned for Zane to enter the elevator first. "I'm interested in hearing the story from your perspective."

Zane waited until they were seated in the restaurant to tell his story. "I came here to spy on Tito Kaysar. The High Council wishes for a follow-up report. He keeps telling the High Council that the research process will take years, and the Council wants to be sure they are hearing the truth."

"They are," Zeke admitted. "Kaysar handed the project to Koren Tafari, who is not a geneticist, but he possesses our best scientific mind. Koren is working diligently, but he also must learn a new field of study. I'd estimate that it's going to take decades before we know anything definitively."

Sipping his wine, Zane processed what he'd just learned. "I figured as much." He sighed. "The High Council was hoping for a rapid timeline. It seems Mr. Granger and Mr. Tafari are not the only members of the Sharp-Winged Tribe to mate with canine shifters. It is also happening in Montevideo. It would be different if the omegas were from a variety of species, perhaps tigers or gargoyles, who are our closest-living relatives, but they are mostly canines. I've heard of a few felines and equines, but it's mostly dog shifters. It is imperative we understand the reasoning behind it and the effect it will have on dragonkind."

Zeke didn't worry about being overheard. In general, anyone who overheard assumed they were engaging in live-action role play. He'd been approached many times by strangers who'd invited him to take part in their games.

Now that he knew the reason behind Zane's visit, Zeke relaxed. "I'll set up a meeting between you and Koren tomorrow. He can catch you up on his progress. Now I'd like to hear about how you came to be in possession of a backpack that wasn't yours."

A tight smile twisted the corners of Zane's mouth. "It is mine."

Scenarios played out in Zeke's mind, but he didn't rush to choose one. "Explain."

"I sat down on the bench next to a man who had nodded off while still sitting up. I set my backpack and briefcase between us, and I called my boss to let him know I had landed. We chatted for about fifteen minutes, and then I picked up my briefcase and backpack—I didn't

31

bring a suitcase—and I set off toward the Draco International building. The next thing I know, this vicious little man is on my back, screaming that I'd stolen his backpack. I fought back. Any injuries he sustained were the result of me defending myself. DI should not pay out a settlement because we are not liable."

Their steak-and-lobster dinners came, and both men dug into the delicious carnivorous feast.

"DI settled to avoid further litigation." Zeke informed Zane of his role. "It's less expensive and cleaner this way."

"I didn't steal anything," Zane insisted. "And the police still have the evidence. They have my briefcase and my backpack."

"They have neither," Zeke informed his dining companion. "The backpack in evidence belonged to Mr. Yardan. It has been returned to him already. DI's lawyers have your briefcase. They were probably intending to return it to you tomorrow, but I'll have them drop it at the hotel tonight." As he talked, he tapped out a text to put the plan in motion. By the time they returned from dinner, Zane's briefcase should be waiting for them.

Gazing across in disbelief, Zane froze. "That was my backpack, Zeke."

Having seen the contents, Zeke did not back down. "Not unless you were carrying around a dancer's leotard, Mr. Yardan's ID, and pictures of his family."

"That's not possible." Zane's gaze unfocused as he thought. "I set it down, took my cell phone from the pocket." His hands moved as he mimed the movements. "Talked to Eduardo." He mumbled a few more things, but Zeke didn't catch them.

"Perhaps yours was stolen when you weren't looking?"

"Maybe." Wrinkles of confusion lined the space between the dark slashes of Zane's eyebrows. "There were many people around. I don't suppose the park is on some kind of city surveillance?"

It was. Zeke nodded. "I'll investigate. In the meantime, you're going to need toiletries and a change of clothes."

"The hotel has supplied most of what I need, though I wouldn't mind stopping at a men's store for a couple shirts."

By the time Zeke had a free moment to return to the hospital, visiting hours were over.

Disappointed, Zeke found a secluded spot to shift into dragon form. His black scales blended into the inky darkness. The light of the full moon reflected from his long body and wings, but to the casual observer, he would look like a dark cloud against the dark sky.

Taking a risk, he glided low, past Marcel's fourth-floor window. But the curtains were drawn and no light peeked out from the edges, meaning his intended omega was likely asleep for the night.

If he was going to heal, he needed his rest.

Zeke returned to where he'd stowed his clothes. They were exactly as he'd left them. Shifters all over the city were in the habit of stashing their clothes when they shifted. To his knowledge, none were ever stolen. Crime in Verdance was virtually non-existent. The fact that Zane's backpack had disappeared was a troubling new development.

Returning to the park, Zeke spent the next hour searching high and low for the missing backpack. He found nothing.

Settling on the edge of the large round fountain the served as a centerpiece of the park, he considered the contacts list on his cell. Marcel had neither called nor texted. He tried not to let disappointment weigh him down as he considered whether he could ask Chay for help. Koren's omega, Chayton Sadler V, was a Labrador shifter, and Labs were known for their nose, among other things.

He called Koren first. "Hey, do you mind if I borrow Chay for an hour or so? I need him to track something for me."

"What kind of danger is involved?"

"None. I'm looking for Zane's missing backpack." Dragons were fighters, and they had great eyesight, but tracking a cold scent was beyond Zeke's purview.

"Let me ask him." Koren muted the phone. When sound returned, he said, "Are you going to come by and get him, or did you want him to meet you somewhere?"

"I'll be right over."

The drive didn't take long. Koren and Chay lived in a posh building not far from the park. When Zeke arrived, Chay was waiting on the sidewalk. He hopped into Zeke's car as soon as it came to a stop.

"I would have come up," Zeke said.

"I needed to get out of there." Chay chuckled. "It's nice to be off baby duty for a while. My parents are coming out next week, and I'm hoping Koren and I can take off for some alone time together."

Zeke did not offer to babysit. Those skills weren't in his wheelhouse. "Glad I could help. What do you need from me to help you track? We can swing by Zane's hotel room and grab anything you need."

"If he'll let me sniff him, that's all I need." Chay leaned across the console and sniffed Zeke's shoulder and neck. "You smell like love. Who's the lucky guy?"

Not fooled by the observation, Zeke snorted. "You cannot discern something like that from smell. You talked to Amar."

"Edgar." Chay's grin grew. "Everybody knows. We're all waiting to meet your mystery man."

Since he wasn't sure about his standing with the aloof Marcel, Zeke brought the conversation back to the matter at hand. He parked and got out of the car. "We're here. Let's get you what you need. Did Koren tell you I'm looking for a backpack?"

"Yes. He said it's probably identical to the one Zane stole from your omega."

"He's not my omega." Zeke's denial came automatically.

Chay made a raspberry noise. "It's a matter of time. The moment I set eyes on Koren, I knew he was the one for me. Your guy got hit on the head, didn't he? Once he's feeling better, he'll come around."

He hadn't called ahead to tell Zane to expect visitors. The alpha lawyer answered the door wearing only his briefs. Chay's nose twitched.

"Hi, Zane. This is Chayton Sadler, Koren's omega. He needs to smell you."

Zane backed up a step. "He... What?"

"Zeke wants me to track where your backpack went. It'll have your scent on it, so I'll need to sniff you a bit." Not at all wary of approaching an alpha uninvited, Chay closed the gap between him and Zane. He sniffed up and down the man's body. When he was done, he stepped back and rubbed his hands together. "Let's do this."

Zane began with his nose wrinkled in disdain, but as he'd held still for the invasion of his personal space, the wrinkle had morphed to curiosity. He regarded Chay speculatively. "You think you can find it?"

Chay shrugged. "I'm pretty good with cold-scent tracking, but I'm better with hot scents."

"I don't know what any of that means." Zane folded his arms over his chest to show that he expected an explanation.

"Cold scents are ones that have been there a while, giving other scents a chance to layer on top of them. Hot scents are fresher, easier to follow. It's more of a hunting thing than a tracking thing." Chay tugged on Zeke's arm. "The faster we get to it, the easier it'll be for me to pick it up."

Zeke took Chay to the park. In the car, Chay shed his clothes and shifted. Flouting the leash laws, Zeke led Chay to the bench where the mixup had taken place. He watched as Chay fluttered around, following and backtracking several times. After a while, Chay barked and took off. His entire demeanor had changed. This was a dog on a mission.

They walked for over a mile before Chay ducked into an alley. He stopped beside a large barrel of trash and lifted his nose into the air. Then he sat on his haunches and shifted to human form. "Backpack is in there, and the scent of the person who stole it goes cold. Maybe they got into a car or something."

Zeke noticed a bus stop nearby. "Or a bus." He pried open the lid on the large trash container and lifted out three bags of trash before he found the backpack in question. Whoever had stolen it had cleaned out the contents. All of Zane's clothes and personal items were gone. To be safe, he checked every pocket.

Since he was naked, Chay shifted back into his canine form for the walk back to the car.

As he dressed, he said, "Sorry I couldn't find your man. But if I come across him, I'll recognize him immediately. We could have a code, like I'll say that the raccoon is in the butterfly bush, or something. Raccoons steal stuff."

Zeke doubted Chay would stumble upon the thief randomly, and he wasn't a fan of speaking in code. However after the favor Chay had done for Zeke, he wasn't about to crush his excitement. "Sure."

He stopped at a bakery to reward Chay with donuts and hot chocolate, and then he took him home before returning to Zane's room.

This time when Zane answered, he wore pajama bottoms. "The canine shifter got a little fresh last time. I thought I'd be better prepared this time."

Zeke went into the suite, his gaze automatically sweeping for signs of danger. "He just needed your scent."

"He's cute."

"He's mated, married, and has two sons."

"Still cute." Zane motioned to the bar, but his gaze remained glued to the item in Zeke's hand. "Can I get you anything?"

"Not tonight." Zeke handed over the backpack. "Chay found it in a trash bin behind a barbershop."

"Is the location significant?" Zane regarded the soiled bag warily. He held it at arm's length as he studied it.

"It was next to a bus stop. I searched it already. It's empty."

Zane sighed. "I'm so glad I carry my most important possessions on my person. I wonder why they targeted me? Mr. Yardan was asleep. I was not."

"You were on your phone. A distracted person is an easy target. Unless you can think of a different reason you were targeted?"

Zane shook his head. "My money was in my pocket, and my important papers are in my briefcase, which nobody took."

"Were you paying attention to your briefcase while you talked?"

"Yes. I was looking for a particular file."

Zeke spread his hands. "It seems like a crime of opportunity. Be vigilant, and you should be fine."

"Thank you for everything you've done tonight."

Chapter 4

Marcel

Holden showed up first thing in the morning. As Marcel poked at rubbery French toast and considered the lukewarm coffee, Holden sailed into the room, a bright smile on his face. "How are you feeling? Are you super sore?"

The day after an injury was often worse than the initial day, and Marcel was feeling every bump and bruise. Determined not to show it, he put his best food forward. He gulped milk from the small carton at the corner of his tray. "I'm okay. Sore, but nothing too bad."

Delight flashed in Holden's blue eyes as he clapped. "Have you tried to walk yet? Maybe your ankle isn't as sprained as we thought."

But it was. Marcel had used a crutch to get to the bathroom. "It's sprained. I'm getting more x-rays today because sometimes breaks don't show up right away, and then there's the concussion."

Letting go of that line of hope, Holden settled into a chair. "Everyone misses you. I talked to Scylla. He said they'll hold your spot for a week."

Break or sprain, Marcel's injury wasn't going to heal in a week. "Only a week?" He sighed. "I knew I didn't have a chance. My luck has run out."

"Oh, I don't know about that. What about the guy with the smoldering gaze who showed up here yesterday? He gave you his phone number."

Marcel had no trouble recalling Zeke Lowry, the ultra-sexy alpha who had brokered a deal while his gaze stripped away Marcel's clothes. "He was sent to handle me. I've been handled, so he's done. Now it'll be lackeys and low-rung lawyers who deal with me. I know how big corporations work."

Holden snorted. "Given the way he was looking at you, he'll be back for a taste. No—a meal."

Now it was Marcel's turn to snort. "I'd love to find a man who is willing to do more than taste. Most of them are all about themselves."

"True." Holden's eyes glazed over as he lost himself in some kind of wistful thought. When he snapped out of it, he said, "I'd give anything to have a woman look at me the way Zeke looked at you yesterday. If you don't want him, there are thousands of other guys who'll take him."

Marcel didn't want Mr. Lowry to find anyone else. He'd liked the way the alpha had looked at him and spoken to him. He liked the way he'd taken charge. He'd liked watching the hospital staff scramble to do Mr. Lowry's bidding.

He just didn't want to be the one scrambling. His fathers had an equal partnership, and that's what he wanted with his eventual mate, not that he was looking anyway. Right now, his career came first. Besides, Ezekiel Lowry was not the kind of man who offered equality. He was the kind who demanded subservience.

"You know what I want in a man? I want one who will get on his knees for me. No—I want one who insists on getting on his knees for me." He'd still be alpha and powerful, but he'd be a generous and considerate lover as well. Little things would matter, like foot rubs and walks in the park. And he'd understand that Marcel's career was important.

The room had gone curiously silent as Marcel mused about his one-day mate. A tingling under his ribs roused him from his reverie, and he looked up to find the object of his never-gonna-happen fantasy standing at the foot of his bed. Marcel felt his eyes widen and his lips part.

Mr. Lowry studied him attentively, as if he'd heard at least a few of Marcel's thoughts. "How are you feeling today?"

"You sound like a nurse." Sarcasm came out when Marcel opened his mouth, a combination of his refusal to cede to Mr. Lowry's stated wishes and a need to establish his independence.

Mr. Lowry frowned, and it was the kind of expression that struck fear into hearts—mainly Marcel's. His heart beat too hard to look over to see if Holden was similarly paralyzed.

Immediately, Marcel regretted his tone and the flippant response. "I mean, I'm okay. I'm sore, but they brought me crutches so I can get around on my own."

Mr. Lowry brought his frown closer. "They didn't put a cast on your arm yet."

"The doctor said I had to wait for the swelling to go down."

The menacing frown melted, and those searing blue eyes focused on Marcel's face. "Oh. Okay, then."

Now Marcel's heart thundered for a different reason. He recognized the heated promise being delivered, and he wanted it as much as he wanted to run away from it. Tearing his gaze from Mr. Lowry's, Marcel forced it to seek new vistas. He noticed that Mr. Lowry was wearing a different suit. This one was charcoal gray shot through with lighter pinstripes. His shirt was crisp and white, and his blue tie guided Marcel's gaze right back to those incredible blue eyes. Mr. Lowry looked positively scrumptious in a suit.

"Mr. Lowry, what brings you back so bright and early?" Holden's loud voice broke the spell binding Marcel to Mr. Lowry.

Mr. Lowry spared Holden the barest of glances. "I came to check on Marcel."

With a lithe grace that most dancers possessed, Holden got to his feet. He rested a hand on Mr. Lowry's arm. "He's fine. I was just leaving to head to rehearsal. I'll walk you out."

Dismissing the blond man in an instant, Mr. Lowry said, "I'm staying."

Holden looked to Marcel, silently communicating that he was willing to stay if Marcel wasn't comfortable being alone with the large, predatory, and utterly handsome alpha male.

Marcel knew Holden couldn't afford to be late. He smiled tightly. "Have a good rehearsal. I'll try to get back on my feet by next week."

Once Holden was gone, Mr. Lowry closed the door. "Your injuries are too severe to heal by next week."

"I know, but Holden said they were holding my position until next week. After that, I'll be fired."

"If you push yourself, you could cause permanent injury that will bar you from dancing for the rest of your life." Mr. Lowry's frown made an encore appearance. "You have an apartment and a stipend that should cover your living expenses. Take the time you need to recover."

He made it sound so simple, as if the opportunity for which he'd worked so hard would still be there when he was ready to take it. But this was a door slamming shut in his face, and it made Marcel more than a little angry. Because he'd gone after a thief, he was going to lose his chance to realize his dreams.

"Easy for you to say. Your job has a little more security than mine."

Mr. Lowry cracked a smile. "You made a pun. I think you'll be fine."

Marcel met the smile that set his heart to beating out of control with a scowl. "I wasn't joking around."

Mr. Lowry perched on the edge of Marcel's bed. The pressure of his hip against Marcel's thigh was shockingly intimate, and the hand he parked on Marcel's thigh was even more so. "I spoke with Scylla, the producer. He's an old friend of mine—a walrus shifter who doesn't like to swim—and he assured me that you'll have a job when you recover. It might not be the same position, but you'll be on the stage."

The riot in his bloodstream prevented Marcel from experiencing the deepest parts of shock. "I— He— How— How did you get him to agree to that?"

"He's a friend. It's a favor."

Favors like that were hard to come by. More than likely, Mr. Lowry meant to protect DI against a lawsuit centered on more than lost wages. Marcel narrowed his eyes. "You paid him."

Mr. Lowry pressed his lips together. "Marcel, you're walking on very thin ice right now."

"Mr. Lowry, are you threatening me?"

He winced at Marcel's use of his honorific title, but he got over it quickly. "Warning you, omega. I did something nice for you. Most people would say thank you." He brushed the pad of his thumb in a half-circle over Marcel's cheek.

Electricity zinged through Marcel, setting his nerves on high alert. Unused to having such a violent chemical reaction to a simple, affectionate touch, Marcel jerked away. He tried not to look at Mr. Lowry directly, but from his peripheral vision, he caught the shades of hurt that manifested in the handsome alpha's eyes and ended in the hard set of his jaw.

Wordlessly, Mr. Lowry left the room.

As the door closed softly behind him, Marcel closed his eyes. He'd never felt that kind of connection before. He'd never had that kind of reaction before. Add to that the trauma he'd endured and the fact that he didn't want Mr. Lowry's kind of alpha in his life, and Marcel's mind was a confused jumble of thoughts, feelings, fear—and yearning.

He wanted Mr. Lowry to come back and touch his face again.

He craved the feel of Mr. Lowry's lips brushing his, the taste of his tongue as he plundered deeper, and the erotic glide of skin against skin.

When he realized Mr. Lowry wasn't coming back, Marcel slowly let out the breath of hope he'd been holding.

That evening, wearing a cast on his arm and an air cast on his leg, Marcel prepared to leave the hospital. Holden was supposed to be there to pick him up, but he'd texted that rehearsals were running late. As he gathered his things, shoving them into his black backpack, a knock sounded at the door.

"I'm decent," he called.

The door opened. "Marcel Yardan?"

He'd been expecting a nurse and hoping for Mr. Lowry. The voice that had him turning around to face the doorway belonged to neither. The man who owned the voice was small in comparison to Mr. Lowry, but average height when compared to regular humans. He had warm brown eyes, and his brown hair had a blond patch over one eye that made him look friendly and playful.

This was a canine shifter.

Marcel hobbled around on his crutch to face his guest. "Yeah. Who are you?"

He man hopped forward, a spring of joy in his step, and stuck out his hand. "Edgar Vidal Granger. Zeke sent me to make sure you got to your new apartment in one piece. He would have come himself, but he's off doing boring business stuff. I only have an hour or so, though. I left my babies with my sister, and they're teething, so she's not going to last long alone with three one-year-olds who are gnawing on everything."

Marcel eyed the omega with a mixture of curiosity and wariness. "You work for Mr. Lowry?"

"Nah. Zeke is BFF's with my husband." Edgar released Marcel's hand and scooped up the backpack. "I'll carry the heavy stuff, and you get to ride in the wheelchair."

Marcel didn't want his backpack out of his sight. "It's light. I can manage."

Edgar tapped his finger on his lips, but he didn't release his hold on the backpack he'd slung over his shoulder. "Zeke said you had an independent streak. Look, I know you're new in town, and you're wary because we're friends with Zane, who did this to you. I get it. But I promise you that Zane didn't mean it. He thought you were some crazy guy trying to steal his backpack, which, by the way, looks exactly like yours. It's the same brand, style, and color. Anyway, Zeke and Chay tracked Zane's backpack to a garbage can, like, a mile away. They found it, but all the stuff inside was missing. Luckily there wasn't much in it except for Zane's clothes and toothbrush and stuff. Zeke thinks Zane was targeted because he was distracted and wasn't paying attention. Because, otherwise, why would someone want Zane's underwear? I mean, he's cute, but come on. Buy him a coffee. It'll go over a lot better than stealing his skivvies."

Replies were unnecessary. Edgar talked a mile a minute, spilling all kinds of facts, opinions, and observations. When the orderly showed up with the wheelchair, Marcel got right in.

Edgar walked alongside them, chatting with the orderly. "Have you worked here long?"

"About seven years."

"Do you like it?" Edgar turned his big eyes on the skinny guy pushing the wheelchair. "I mean, it's a lot of hard work."

"I like working with people, helping them feel better." The orderly's smile came through in his tone.

"That's fantastic. Marcel is a dancer. I can't imagine doing that either. I'm not very graceful. Amar, my husband, says I'm a walking hazard. He says if there's trouble out there, I'll find it."

Marcel found himself unable to swallow a quiet chuckle. Edgar's effusive love of everything and everyone was infectious. He could see where it made up for his talkative nature.

They loaded Marcel into an SUV. As he waited for Edgar to get in the driver's seat, he glanced in the back. It was full of baby accessories, like car seats and toys, stray diapers and lone nuggets of dry cereal. The smell of babies was overpowering.

Edgar got inside and breathed deeply. A huge grin broke out on his face. "I'm sorry about the mess, but with three little ones, sometimes cleaning gets shoved to the back burner."

"It's fine," Marcel said. The idea of having kids at this point in his life made Marcel feel like he was suffocating. It would mean giving up his dreams, and he was not prepared to do that. It was another reason to keep Mr. Lowry at arm's length. "So, you're a dog shifter?"

"Yes. Tibetan Terrier. I'm a small, yippy dog, and a petite, talkative man." Edgar giggled. "My husband is a big, quiet man. Opposites attract. Kind of like with you and Zeke."

"Mr. Lowry?" Marcel's breath caught. He hadn't behaved in a way that would lead a stranger to assume there was anything between them. There wasn't.

"Oh, yeah. He said you won't call him by his first name. It's driving him nuts." Edgar giggled again. "I've never seen anyone rattle Zeke the way you have."

"We're not, um, we're not...together."

"Not yet." Edgar favored Marcel with a smile as he merged with traffic outside of the hospital. "Zeke's a good guy—trustworthy, dependable, smart."

"Demanding," Marcel murmured.

"Well, he's an alpha. Of course he's demanding and bossy. That doesn't mean he's unreasonable. He's also romantic. He was the first one who encouraged Amar to pursue me." Edgar's smile turned dreamy.

Something about Edgar urged Marcel to confide in him. "I don't like most alphas. I'm not a submissive omega."

"That's good. Zeke needs someone who'll stand up to him." Edgar turned into a parking garage with a sign that warned it was for tenants only. He swiped a card on the reader, and the gate opened to admit the car.

"You live here?"

"Yes," Edgar confirmed. "We'll be neighbors, sort of. We're on the top floor, penthouse. You're on the ground floor. This way, I'll be around if you need help or if you just want some company."

Marcel emerged from the parked car, holding onto the body for balance while Edgar extracted his crutches from the back. He wondered if living in the same building as Zeke's BFF, as Edgar had indicated, meant he'd run into Zeke a lot. The thought left Marcel with a confusing mix of feelings. While part of him craved the alpha's attention, another part was terrified he'd never dance again.

An elevator took them from the underground parking structure to the first floor of the apartment building.

"I haven't seen inside your apartment." Edgar's chatter continued. "So the décor might be frightful, depending on who decorated it. I swear, some of these dragons fell in love with the wrong designs. I know it's small, but it's more than big enough for just you. It has two bedrooms, so you could probably use one as a dance studio. If it's like my place, it has beautiful hardwood floors." He glanced back at Marcel's crutches, noting the rubber tips on the bottom. "You'll be fine."

At the door to the apartment, Edgar handed a set of keys to Marcel. Marcel took them, noting the smaller key for the mailbox and the larger one for the deadbolt. "What's the third key for?"

"Access to the building. We don't have a doorman or concierge all the time like some of the buildings do." Edgar motioned to the door. "Are you nervous? I probably shouldn't have said it might be decorated like a Nineteenth Century bordello."

Unsure if his escort was kidding, Marcel shot a sidelong glance to Edgar. "You didn't say that."

"Okay, good. I meant to keep that to myself." Edgar clapped. "Go on. Open it up."

Marcel fit the key into the lock and opened the door to reveal a narrow entryway with a closet, and a hall that led to the right. He flipped the light switch, and he hobbled down the hall. After a few feet, it opened to the left, revealing a good-sized living room. The kitchen and dining area were off the living room, each separated by wide, curved openings.

The hallway continued past the kitchen, where Marcel noted another entrance, to a pair of bedrooms with a bathroom between them.

The décor was nondescript—cream walls and furniture in shades of brown. A few paintings lent the majority of the color to the space. It wasn't depressing, yet it stopped short of cheerful.

"The layout isn't bad," Edgar noted. "Big rooms." He crossed the living room to a sliding door. "You have a private patio."

"Yeah," Marcel allowed. "It's fine."

It was the fricking Four Seasons compared to his previous accommodations. For a brief second, he felt a little sorry for his fellow dancers crammed six to a room a quarter the size of this living room. Then he sighed. He'd give anything to be with them right now.

Edgar's hand on his shoulder roused him from his wistful thoughts. "You'll feel better after a soak in your own bathtub and a good night's sleep in your new bed."

Marcel wasn't inclined to agree, but he kept his brooding thoughts to himself. "Thanks. I can take it from here."

For the first time, Edgar appeared uncertain, like he wasn't sure if he'd done something wrong. "Um, okay. Sure." He set Marcel's backpack on the sofa. "If you need anything, let me know. We have extra toothbrushes and whatnot. Don't hesitate to call." He pulled a card from his back pocket. "This is Amar's card, but I wrote our home number and my cell on the back."

Marcel took it from him. "Thanks, again. I appreciate you taking the time to drive a stranger home from the hospital."

"Sure." Edgar's hesitation was still there, but instead of the anxiety, he radiated confusion.

Before he could move to leave, the sound of the front door opening captured both men's attention. Marcel immediately recognized Mr. Lowry's scent mixed in with two others.

"James, put those bags in the kitchen. Neven, take those to the bathroom." Mr. Lowry's authoritative voice sailed through the space and claimed a spot near Marcel's libido.

Two men hurried past the opening to the living room. Marcel watched as the kitchen light came on, and a man set a whole bunch of cloth shopping bags on the counter. Immediately he began unpacking them. Meanwhile, rustling noises came from the bathroom.

Mr. Lowry's imposing figure appeared in the doorway. Until now, Marcel had considered it a wide opening. Given the way the alpha shifter filled the space, he revised his opinion. That penetrating cerulean gaze found Marcel with unerring accuracy.

The predator was in the house.

Then his gaze swung to the other omega. "Edgar, you arrived sooner than I expected."

Edgar parked a hand on his hip and huffed. "I told you I didn't have time to take him out to dinner."

"I know, I just... Never mind. Thank you for picking him up."

Mollified, Edgar patted Mr. Lowry on the arm. "I'll see you tomorrow night, seven sharp."

Mr. Lowry nodded. "Good night, Edgar. Give my best to Grange."

While these pleasantries were happening, the people in the kitchen and bathroom finished their tasks. They stood off to the side, waiting for Mr. Lowry's attention, which he promptly gave them.

"You're finished?"

"Yes, Mr. Lowry."

"Thank you."

The pair exited, and that's when Marcel noticed Edgar had gone as well. Now he was alone with Mr. Lowry.

Gesturing to the kitchen, Marcel said, "What was that about?"

"It occurred to me that you might need staples, since everything you own fits into a backpack. You'll find food in the kitchen and personal hygiene products in the bathroom. The apartment already has non-perishable supplies, like dishes, cutlery, and towels."

Marcel wasn't sure how to respond. "This comes out of my monthly allowance?"

"No." A brief frown marred Mr. Lowry's chin.

Limping closer on his crutches because he couldn't resist the tempting scent emanating from Mr. Lowry, Marcel scowled. Mostly, he was upset because he had the urge to rub his body on the sexy alpha, and fighting instinct was never fun. "I'm not going to have sex with you, Mr. Lowry."

Those eyes coolly assessed Marcel. Mr. Lowry's nostrils flared, but other than that, he didn't seem to have a reaction. "I don't recall offering, Marcel."

That voice washed over Marcel, the utterance of his name like a sensual caress. "Then why would you go out of your way to be here when you knew I was coming?"

Mr. Lowry's lips pressed together, a subtle tell that should have been a warning. "As you heard me tell Edgar, I thought it would take longer to discharge you. I had planned to be in and out before you arrived."

Marcel didn't like hearing that Mr. Lowry had intended to avoid him. Instinct warred with his better sense, creating a level of turmoil Marcel had never before experienced. He should have been ecstatic that the alpha was honoring Marcel's professed wishes. When an omega pledged himself to an alpha, that alpha had expectations. He'd expect Marcel to quit his job, stay home, and raise the children. Many omegas wanted that kind of life, but Marcel did not.

He wanted to dance on the stage. He wanted to hear the thunder of applause and soak in the adoration of the audience.

He put a hand to his temple in an attempt to block the discord in his head.

Mr. Lowry's arm slid around Marcel's waist. "Let me help you to the sofa. Do you need a pill or something? I don't know what they sent you home from the hospital with."

He let Mr. Lowry guide him to the couch, and he luxuriated in the feel of the strong man's hands on his body. Marcel's ankle throbbed, reminding him of the reason he was in this predicament, but he wasn't keen on polluting his body with unnecessary medications. "The anti-inflammatory."

"Where is it?"

Now that he was at the sofa, Marcel opened up his backpack and pulled out the prescription bottle. "Can you get me a glass of water?"

In half a minute, Mr. Lowry returned with a glass.

Marcel took it from him. "Thanks."

"Have you eaten?"

"I had dinner at the hospital."

Mr. Lowry stacked throw pillows on Marcel's right side. "It's been a while since I've broken an arm, but I remember that you're supposed to keep it elevated."

Marcel set his arm on the pillows. "You don't have to keep being nice to me."

"I'm trying to get into your pants, remember?"

The dry delivery had Marcel's head whipping up to look at Mr. Lowry so quickly he pulled a muscle in his shoulder. Before he thought to temper his reaction, he felt a smile spread across his features. "You have a sense of humor."

"Yes. And a temper."

Marcel lowered his lashes coyly, allowing himself to enjoy this banter. "Is that a warning, Mr. Lowry?"

"No, cupcake, but this is."

With that, the alpha's lips closed over Marcel's. The action was unexpected and unwelcome, and yet Marcel would rather die than pull away. He recalled the last time he'd rejected when Mr. Lowry had offered something of himself. Vestiges of pain lanced through his heart, and Marcel knew he'd rather face a real dagger than see the hurt in Mr. Lowry's eyes and feel the emptiness of his absence. More than that, his canine was finally happy.

Mr. Lowry's strong mouth moved over Marcel's soft lips, a gentle coaxing that had Marcel moaning as he parted his lips to invite the alpha deeper.

Rather than accept what was offered, Mr. Lowry ended the kiss. He straightened up and stepped back. Marcel blinked at the transformation. Gone was the man who'd teased him with a kiss, and in his place was a man with a firm set to his jaw and a cold remoteness in his eyes.

Mr. Lowry gestured to a lever on the side of the couch. "The ends of the sofa recline. You really should keep your ankle elevated as well."

Marcel's mind was not on his throbbing ankle. Other parts of him throbbed, like his lips and his cock. "How was that a warning?"

By way of response, Mr. Lowry flashed a devilish smile, revealing a cute set of dimples.

"That's not an answer. You can't just kiss me and not explain yourself." With an aggravated grunt, Marcel pounded his good fist on the arm of the sofa.

"Awww, cupcake. You're so cute when you're angry."

With a start, Marcel realized that Mr. Lowry was calling him out. It was true Marcel had pushed Mr. Lowry's buttons because it brought him pleasure. "Do not call me by that ridiculous name."

"I will stop when you declare a cease-fire."

"So this is what we're doing? We're just going to do and say things to piss each other off—until what?"

"Cease-fire, cupcake." His maddening grin grew. "I'll play your game for as long as you want, and I'll give you fair warning—I give as good as I get."

Unbidden and unwanted, a thrill ran through Marcel. He had the sense he was in over his head, but a reckless part of him didn't care— and the part of him that yearned for Mr. Lowry's touch cheered. Rather than put his leg up, Marcel leaned forward. "You give as good as you get? Prove it." Before Marcel knew what he was doing, he took Mr. Lowry's hand, and he set it on his cock. The thing stirred to life, nudging the alpha's hand.

The grin melted from Mr. Lowry's face, transforming into a heavy-lidded expression that failed to warn Marcel of his intention. He knelt down, which put his lips at the perfect height for kissing.

Marcel watched the tip of Mr. Lowry's tongue peek out and flick against his lower lip. It was forked, and his eyes had transformed. Now they were dark with even darker slits for pupils. It was sexy as hell, and the few remaining pieces of Marcel's brain that still worked short-circuited.

"Holy fuck, you are a dragon. Or a really big lizard."

"Tread lightly, omega." With that, he closed his mouth over Marcel's, capturing it for a kiss that seared clear to his toes.

Primal need controlled his behavior. Marcel's shifter side was firmly in charge. He spread his legs wider, welcoming his alpha closer to his core.

Mr. Lowry moaned. One hand massaged Marcel's cock, while the other grasped the back of his neck to hold him still. The kiss went on and on, and when Mr. Lowry finally broke away, Marcel was a writhing mass of need.

Sometime during the kiss, Mr. Lowry had lowered Marcel's pants, exposing his thick cock. His hand pumped slowly, and then he bent his head down, blocking Marcel's view.

A tongue lapped at the sensitive underside of the crown before roaming the length. Once he'd wet the shaft, Mr. Lowry's hot mouth closed around Marcel's throbbing cock.

With a gasp, Marcel lifted his hips, thrusting into Mr. Lowry's wet warmth.

A large hand settled on his thigh, holding him down as the alpha's head bobbed up and down. He found himself lifted and turned so that he lay on the sofa, and his pants were gone.

Somehow Mr. Lowry's tongue was everywhere, caressing and wrapping around Marcel's thick member. His free hand wrapped around Marcel's balls, and a finger invaded his anus. Pleasure, insistent and bright, zinged through his body. Before long, a climax loomed. Thunderous waves crashed into him as his orgasm exploded.

As he came down, he found himself cradled in Mr. Lowry's arms. The big man held him tenderly, murmuring assurances and pressing kisses to Marcel's temple. All the while, he played gentle caresses along Marcel's hip and thigh.

His canine wasn't as settled as Marcel hoped it would be. In fact, the interlude only made it want more, and it remained firmly in control. Tipping his face up, Marcel nibbled Mr. Lowry's lower lip. "More," he moaned.

"You're hurt," Mr. Lowry's voice rumbled through Marcel's consciousness, setting off a dozen riots.

Feverish with a desire he'd never before felt, Marcel moaned. "Please."

"I'll be careful of your ankle." His strangled assurance revealed that Mr. Lowry was at the mercy of his shifter every bit as much as Marcel was. He got to his feet, lifting Marcel with him.

Marcel wiggled until Mr. Lowry let him wrap his legs around the alpha's waist. He tore at his mate's shirt, ridding him of his tie and opening most of the buttons before they made it to the bed.

Mr. Lowry lowered Marcel down, somehow undressing the rest of the way as he did so. His movements were a graceful blur. Seconds later, he stood next to the bed. Long, sinewy muscles corded his body into sculpted perfection, but he seemed entirely unaware of exactly how sexy he was. "You're sure?"

Faced with naked magnificence and at the mercy of his animal, Marcel nodded. "I need to feel you inside me."

Mr. Lowry settled between Marcel's legs. Automatically, Marcel lifted his knees, spreading them wider. The alpha rained kisses on Marcel's chest, arms, and shoulders. Alternating with stinging bites and soothing licks, he tracked pinpricks of pleasure in his wake. By the time he made it to the sensitive places on Marcel's neck, the omega was a writhing mass of need.

He lifted his knees higher. "Now, please. I need you now."

Mr. Lowry reached between them, and Marcel felt the large, blunt tip of the alpha's cock at his entrance. He pressed forward, easing into Marcel's body.

For his part, Marcel felt split open, a rift that allowed insane amounts of bliss to travel along his veins. His heart beat faster, and he lifted his hips to urge his lover deeper.

The alpha's cock slid home. Mr. Lowry paused, his body a mass of tense, trembling passion. "Are you okay?"

"Perfect," Marcel said. Nothing in his life had ever felt so fucking perfect. Even more than dancing, being joined to this man made him feel complete and whole, as if this was the whole point of existing.

Mr. Lowry moved in him, his pace increasing as sexy grunts and moans escaped from between his luscious lips. Every few thrusts, he pressed another kiss to Marcel's lips. The whole time, he held Marcel prisoner with his penetrating gaze. Something inexorable passed between them, and Marcel's canine whined.

Marcel reached between them, and he took his cock—hard once again—in hand.

A sensual smile played about Mr. Lowry's lips. "You're going to come with me."

It was an order, a directive he couldn't conceive of disobeying. "Yes."

"Now."

With a shout, Mr. Lowry slammed deep as he climaxed. Warm jets of semen bathed Marcel's insides, triggering Marcel's orgasm. His seed spilled on his stomach, and the world went black.

A little while later, he opened his eyes to find his body clean and tucked into the covers. A light from the hall hinted at Mr. Lowry's whereabouts.

Marcel got out of bed, careful to put his weight on his good ankle. His clothes and crutches were in the other room, so he wrapped the blanket around his body and clung to the wall for support. He found the alpha in the bathroom. He was mostly dressed, though his pants and shirt hung open.

When he spied Marcel in the threshold, a huge smile broke out over his features. "I thought you might be out for the night."

Marcel looked the alpha up and down. "A great time to make your escape."

Mr. Lowry opened his mouth to speak, but Marcel beat him to the punch.

"Look, Mr. Lowry, let me be perfectly clear."

Mr. Lowry leaned against the sink and crossed his arms. He had a wary look in his brilliant blue eyes. "Go for it."

This wasn't good. Images of domestic bliss winged through Marcel's head, shoving aside his dream of being a dancer, and that gave him the courage to plow ahead. "I don't care that you're leaving. It would be awkward if you stayed. We've only known each other for a day."

"I wasn't leaving. I was going to run upstairs to Amar's place and grab the overnight bag I keep there."

That didn't make Marcel feel better. Now that his animal had been sated, his better sense was back in control. And his better sense would let nothing stand in the way of achieving his ultimate goal. He took a deep breath and gritted his teeth against the unpleasantness to come. "I don't want to be your omega. I came to Verdance prepared to work hard and make a name for myself in the theater, and that's what I'm going to do. I'm not going to let an accident or an alpha stop me from pursuing my dreams."

Chapter 5

Zeke

Zeke struggled not to frown. In fact, he controlled his face so well that it betrayed no hint of the way Marcel's declaration gutted him.

His omega didn't want him?

He'd been prepared to accept that his omega was likely a canine shifter. He'd been prepared to break the news to his parents. He'd been prepared to have offspring—hybrid offspring—a century or two earlier than he'd originally planned.

He had not anticipated his omega rejecting him outright.

By some miracle, he controlled his temper. "You think I would stop you from pursuing your dreams?"

"I know you would."

Zeke chafed at that. "You have no idea what I would or wouldn't do."

"You're an alpha, and you're an apex predator. It's not hard to connect the dots."

It appeared they were nowhere near a cease-fire. Zeke heaved a sigh. He'd been reticent to sleep with Marcel so quickly, but the omega had begged. He found he was a sucker for his canine's whine. With that one sound, Marcel was going to be able to get him to do anything.

He realized he'd fucked up by not waiting. He should have resisted temptation a while longer. Recognizing it was best to let Marcel have this one, Zeke retreated. "I'm not playing connect-the-dots, cupcake. However, I recognize that you're still feeling poorly. We will continue this discussion later."

Zeke knew he should stay and talk it out, but the fury pumping through his veins wouldn't let him attempt more small kindnesses. Without a further word, he left.

Out on the street, he ran, not caring that his suit shredded as he shifted, and he took flight in full view on a public street.

In a fit of rage and pain, he flew. Not caring which direction the winds took him, he glided on currents and fought against prevailing winds when they got in his way. The recklessness of his actions didn't matter. A lifetime of admonitions against revealing the presence of dragons to humankind ceased to be a factor. He'd stopped thinking at all. His primal nature was, once again, in control.

High up in the mountains, he'd find a cave suitable for building a nest to raise young. He'd bring his omega here, where they'd be

protected from danger and isolated from the outside world—just like his ancestors used to do.

Having a purpose, his brain focused on that task. As he calmed, his laser-sharp vision roamed the snow-covered crags in search of a place to raise his young. It needed to be protected from weather and predators, though no creature who wanted to live would challenge a dragon or its young.

He spotted a possible location, and as he dove to check it out, he became aware that he wasn't alone in the late-afternoon sky. Three dragons surrounded him. Their sky blue coloring indicated Ice-Breathers.

Immediately on the defensive, he banked east, away from the location he was scouting. He hadn't even claimed the nest, and already he was deflecting attention from it.

One dragon came closer, and Zeke let loose with a stream of fire. An expert flamethrower, he aimed the warning shot across the dragon's nose. The would-be attacker veered off to avoid being singed, and the other two closed in.

Familiar with this style of attack, Zeke rolled and curled, turning himself sideways in midair to aim fire at one Ice-Breather while he used his razor-sharp talons to battle the other. Taking on two dragons was a feat in and of itself. Taking on three was lunacy.

If ever there was a day when Ezekiel Lowry was poised for lunacy, this was it.

The third Ice-Breather joined in the attack. The foursome wrestled in the sky, flying through the atmosphere in a ball of fire and clutching talons. Like Sharp-Winged dragons, Ice-Breathers had thick scales and sharp talons. It was difficult to cause damage, but not impossible.

Zeke used his wings as well, the protruding bones at the apex and ends of his wings acting as secondary talons to slice and stab.

The Ice-Breathers countered his fiery breath with subzero bursts, and the trio soon battled Zeke to the point of exhaustion. He found himself on the ground with three Ice-Breathers on top of him. Huge rocks cradled his belly and trapped his legs, rendering his talons useless.

What brings you to Pleasance, Sharp-Winged trespasser? A clear, blue iris surrounded the lizard slit of a pupil, and it studied him dispassionately.

Zeke hadn't known he was anywhere near Pleasance. The Sharp-Winged tribe steered clear of Pleasance unless invited, spying, or looking for a fight. The way Zeke had flown in, the Ice-Breathers had every reason to believe he'd come looking for a fight.

And they'd obliged.

Ezekiel Lowry.

At the utterance of his name, Zeke's primal brain ceded control to his better sense. The frantic glaze melted from his consciousness, and he forced his body to relax even though two Ice-Breathers still restrained him. He looked toward the dragon who'd thought his name.

It took him a moment, but he identified Lajos Edison, his counterpart at Gliding Principles. *Lajos. Apologies. I didn't realize I was near Pleasance.*

Bullshit. Lajos' disbelief was understandable. Only an idiot wouldn't know where he was going. *You came here looking for trouble.*

He'd done that before, usually to deflect while Koren or another Sharp-Winged dragon stole tech or research. Both tribes made a habit of stealing from one another. Koren's collaboration with Anshu Bray over genetic research was the first time they'd peacefully worked together.

If you let me up, I'll shift. It was a peace offering. Just as he was not much of a threat when there were three of them and one of him, he was even less of a threat in human form. He'd be alone and naked, utterly defenseless.

Lajos motioned to his companions, and the duo slowly released their hold on Zeke. Following through on his promise, Zeke shifted.

The first thing he noticed was the freezing temperature. Though it was late fall, this high in the mountains, it was always winter. In dragon form, the temperature was balmy and pleasant. In human form, it was fucking cold. He shivered, but he refrained from crossing his arms.

Lajos shifted as well, but his lieutenants did not. A typical Ice-Breather, Lajos had straw-colored hair and pale blue eyes. Looking closer, Zeke found distinguishing characteristics—a sharp line to his jaw, thick lips, and a scar along the inner part of his right thigh. Due to the cold, his balls were every bit as shriveled as Zeke's, so he didn't make judgments there.

Stepping closer, Lajos held Zeke's gaze. "No Sharp-Winged dragon comes here with pureness of intent."

Zeke nodded, ceding the point. "Nevertheless, I didn't come here with any kind of intent. I've had a bad day, and I took flight to clear my head. I didn't pay attention to where I was headed."

Lajos circled wide, stalking to establish his superior position in the conversation. "That is unlike you. I remember you from school, Ezekiel Lowry. You were methodical and hyperaware, just as I am. It's why we have both risen so quickly to the top of our profession."

Most Ice-Breathers attended the same college as the Sharp-Winged dragons. Though they hadn't become friends, they'd been aware of one another. The same could be said for Silver-Winged and Fire-Breathers. For the first time, Zeke wondered why they'd avoided forming friendships. They were all dragons.

Suddenly the tribal lines that divided them seemed arbitrary. Even so, they were etched deep in all their minds. Zeke didn't think Lajos would have the same shift in thinking.

He inhaled deeply, letting the cold air fill his lungs. When he exhaled, he was once again completely in control of his faculties. "You know how we're in the midst of an omega shortage?"

Lajos' eyes narrowed. "Anshu said he'd made a deal with the Sharp-Winged Tribe to find him an alpha." His nostrils flared, and he peered closer at Zeke, his calculating gaze raking over Zeke's body. "He is a good man. You will treasure him."

Anshu Bray was the single dragon omega any of them knew about, but for some reason, no alpha wanted to mate with him. Zeke had met Anshu several times, and he'd never felt a connection with the omega. Instead, he'd fallen hard for a canine omega who wanted nothing to do with him because it might interfere with his aspirations to become a dancer.

A fucking dancer.

Zeke had seen people dance, but he'd never felt the need to try it for himself.

He shook his head, not to negate Lajos' order, but to deny his intent to marry Anshu. "I have found my omega. He is not Anshu."

It was an accurate statement. If Anshu was his destined mate, the omega would not have had sex with Zeke and then kicked him to the curb. Anshu Bray was no fool. Marcel Yardan, on the other hand, well, arguments could be made in that direction.

A moment ago, Lajos had relaxed a miniscule amount. Now his alert tension returned. "Then why are you here?"

Zeke closed his eyes. "Sincerely—it was a mistake. Things are not going smoothly with my omega, and I just needed to get away. I didn't trust myself to be around him in my condition." He shivered violently. "Look, my head is on straight once again. How about I head home, and we forget about this incident?"

Lajos stared. Zeke knew what his counterpart was thinking because he knew what he'd be thinking if he was in Lajos' shoes. There was nothing he could say to hurry the process, and any attempt he made to plead his case would merely cause Lajos to doubt his story.

Finally Lajos crossed his arms. "Your omega is a canine shifter?"

Information was power, and Zeke's training cautioned him against revealing intel. "Lajos, you and I are not friends. I don't wish to discuss my personal life with you."

"It's happening here as well." Lajos nodded to the dragon to Zeke's left. "Jagger has recently mated with a canine omega, as have two other Ice-Breathers. Three female alphas have recently taken up with equine shifters, and a Silver-Winged acquaintance has mated with a feline shifter. Anshu is taking it all rather hard."

"I'm sorry." Truly, he was. Anshu seemed like a nice enough guy. "I know Anshu and Koren are working toward understanding this phenomenon."

"I don't care about it," Lajos said. "I've known Anshu my whole life. We grew up together. I always assumed the day would come when I would take him as my omega mate, but when he tried to kiss me, my dragon protested—vehemently."

This was of no concern to Zeke. He thought about his idea that tribal allegiances didn't have to prevent them from forging closer relationships. "It seems like you do care about their research. No doubt you'd like to know why your dragon will probably imprint on a non-dragon omega instead of a perfectly good dragon omega."

Pale lightning flashed through Lajos' eyes. "I cannot find an omega before Anshu finds an alpha. I can't do that to him."

Zeke's dragon rebelled at the idea of having an omega who wasn't Marcel. He fought against the urge to take a step back. "Koren is looking. He's met with Rock-Shaper and Silver-Winged dragons. He is working on arranging meetings between several interested alphas and Anshu."

Politics had to be navigated. Clan identity clashed with a desperate need to find omega dragons.

Lajos motioned over his shoulder. "You will come peacefully back to Pleasance."

Studying Lajos through a shrewd lens, Zeke realized that Lajos had more to discuss, but he didn't intend for Zeke to freeze to death while that happened. A half hour later, he found himself in front of a fireplace, listening to the crackle of burning wood as the warmth of the flames chased the stiffness from his fingers. It was better than a jail cell or interrogation room.

Lajos had dismissed Jagger and Cezar, though the pair waited on the rooftop in case circumstances changed, and Zeke decided to become a threat.

He wore sweats and a cotton shirt, courtesy of Lajos. The two were of a similar height, though Lajos had the thinner build of his tribe.

"Can I borrow your phone?"

Lajos called from the kitchen. "Landline is in here. Cell phones have spotty reception this high in the mountains."

Zeke reluctantly left the glow of the fire. He dialed a number. "Amar, I left all my stuff on the sidewalk in front of your building."

Puzzled silence greeted him. Then Amar cleared his throat. "Any particular reason you're calling from a Pleasance number?"

"I'm in Pleasance." He did not go into detail. "Don't ask, okay? Just get my wallet, keys, and cell."

"Are you in danger?"

"No. I'm fine. We'll talk tomorrow." He wasn't fine, and he knew his friend knew that.

"Zeke, I can be there in an hour."

"It's fine. I'm having a drink with Lajos Edison."

"I thought you were having dinner with Marcel? Edgar said he'd left the two of you alone."

"He did." Zeke was glad Edgar hadn't been there to witness Marcel's rejection. He could stand a lot of things from the effusive omega, but not pity. "I'm going to go now. Thanks for getting my things. I'll be by in the morning to collect them."

He didn't figure on getting out of Lajos' apartment until the predawn hours.

When he ended the call, he turned to find Lajos offering a mug. "Irish coffee. It's strong. You look like you need something strong."

Zeke wasn't sure whether Lajos referred to the icy sojourn on a rocky mountain outcrop or Zeke's emotional state. He opted for the former. "Thanks. It was damned cold out there."

He followed Lajos back into the living room, and the pair settled on chairs in front of the fire. It was quite a domestic scene, completely at odds with the way he'd envisioned his night a few hours ago when he'd taken flight.

They sipped in silence for a few moments, and then Lajos said, "I don't expect you to confide in me. As you mentioned, we are not friends. However, I think the time has come for us to become acquaintances."

Zeke agreed, but years of rivalry meant that instant trust wouldn't be part of their new association. "What brought this on? An hour ago, you were ready to kill me."

Lajos waved his hand dismissively. "If I wanted to kill you, you'd be dead. When security spotted you flying around, I will admit I was surprised and puzzled. Your flying pattern indicated you were searching for something."

This was a fishing expedition, and Zeke was never going to admit his intention. It had been a wholly primal and inhumane reaction. And so he went with something safe that confirmed the narrative he'd been feeding Lajos. "I was searching for things not found outside myself, like restraint and perspective."

"Because you had a fight with your omega?"

If it had merely been a fight, Zeke would have won—or at least he'd have arrived at an acceptable compromise. He'd never been handed an ultimatum by someone on whom he couldn't use violence to disagree. "Yeah," he muttered. "A fight."

"Omegas can be headstrong." Lajos sipped his coffee and stared into the fire. "An alpha must be strong enough to wait them out."

Zeke didn't know how much patience he could muster for a stubborn man who refused to even acknowledge that, with one primal act, they'd cemented their bond. He looked over at Lajos, noting his pensive expression. "You have an omega?"

"Yes. And no." Lajos sighed. "I cannot be with him until Anshu is settled, but my omega is not sympathetic to my plight. He won't return my calls, and when I knock on his door, he refuses to open it."

It was unlikely Marcel would answer the door if Zeke knocked or answer the phone if Zeke called. He lifted his mug and took a swig. "Mine isn't submissive either. He wants to be a dancer, and he thinks I'll stop him from achieving his dreams."

"You will," Lajos said. "Alphas like us want an omega who will manage our lives and our children. It will leave him no time for a career."

Zeke thought about Edgar and Chay, omegas who were happy to be house-husbands. Serving Amaricio and Koren made each man happy and fulfilled. Zeke couldn't deny wanting an omega who focused his whole life on his alpha.

He downed the rest of his coffee, luxuriating in the burn of hot liquid mixed with Irish whiskey. "I'm fucked."

"We both are." Lajos chuckled. "I brought you here in the hopes of getting you drunk enough to agree to take Anshu back with you. Koren Tafari can collaborate with him much easier in Verdance. I'd hoped you might see an opportunity for Draco International to own the data and whatever develops from it. And, of course, it will put him in Tafari's cross-hairs, which might spur him into finding an alpha for Anshu all the faster."

Shocked that Lajos would consider robbing Gliding Principles of valuable research and their top scientific mind, Zeke took his time thinking through a response. "It would solve your personal problem, but I can't take the chance that the rest of the Ice-Breathers would be on board with losing Anshu from their tribe."

"You'd be surprised." Lajos grimaced. "We have the only omega dragon in existence, and nobody here wants anything to do with him. Having him here is distressing for all Ice-Breathers." Sitting forward, Lajos pinched the bridge of his nose. "I feel like an ass for suggesting it—because it does simplify my life—but the fact remains that Anshu is unhappy here. He's a good man. He deserves to be happy."

Zeke thought about what it was like to be rejected by someone who should want him, and he felt boundless sympathy for the unwanted omega.

"I'll take him," Zeke said. "If he's willing, I'll take him back to Verdance with me."

Chapter 6

Marcel

"If I got rid of the dining room furniture, it would make a great practice space." Marcel tapped his finger on his lower lip as he thought aloud. Right now, he was desperate for anything that would take his mind off a rather large problem that had cropped up after Zeke's one and only visit.

Holden came in from the kitchen, a damp dish towel thrown over one shoulder. In exchange for the second bedroom, Holden had offered to take care of the cooking and cleaning. While he was a good cook, his cleaning habits were not up to Marcel's standards, and so when Holden was at dance practice, Marcel cleaned whatever he could get to.

In the month since his accident, his ankle had almost healed. He no longer needed crutches, but he found if he stayed on it too long, then it swelled up. Physical therapy was scheduled to begin in the next week. His arm was still in a cast, but even that was almost completely healed.

Hands on hips, Holden surveyed the area. "If you push your recovery, you could permanently damage your ankle, and then you'll never dance again." He looked over at Marcel. "Of course, with the way you've pudged out, it's going to take even longer to get back in shape, so maybe you should be doing some exercises."

In the past month, Marcel had not only continued eating as if he was burning off vast amounts of calories dancing each day, but he'd stepped up his game. He had cravings for things like sweet potato mash smothered in cinnamon and butter. A smokehouse grill two streets over sold it by the quart, and a $2000 stipend could buy a lot of mash.

He refrained from putting his hand on the growing bump on his abdomen. It seemed as if Zeke Lowry had left him with more than a fond memory and a yearning for more.

"I wouldn't push it, but I could do stretches and strength training." Marcel had no plans to rush his recovery. Though he was anxious to get back into the dance studio, he kept the bigger picture in mind. Holden was correct in his caution.

Not only that, but now he had to figure out how in the fucking world he was going to balance having a baby with launching himself into stardom. When he'd first realized he was pregnant, he'd wanted to hand the child over to Zeke and go his separate way. But the longer the child grew inside him, the more attached he became.

How was it possible to both love and resent someone he had yet to meet? And his emotions were so extreme there was no way he could apply logic to the situation.

Sniffling, he beat back tears that threatened a deluge yet again.

Holden gestured to the space in front of the fireplace. "If you moved the chairs, table, and rug, you could use that space."

On cold nights, Marcel loved to sit in front of the fire. He did not, however, dine at the formal table. He and Holden either ate in the kitchen or in front of the television. He didn't want to lose his favorite space. "No, the table needs to go. I just don't know where to put it."

"I'm sure if you contact Zeke Lowry, he'd take care of it for you."

At the mention of the alpha's name, Marcel closed his eyes against the wave of longing that swept over him. Marcel had not seen or heard from Mr. Lowry since the day he'd told him he'd never be his omega. He missed the dragon shifter every bit as much as he dreaded the prospect of seeing him again.

Though Zeke had heeded his wish to not push for a relationship, Marcel still ran into the sexy shifter in passing. It seemed Zeke had a standing dinner reservation at the Granger residence at least once a week, and he could be found coming and going at other times as well. Whenever Marcel ran into Zeke, he'd nod in acknowledgment and continue on his way. Neither of them uttered a word, and no smoldering looks passed between them.

"I don't want to bother him." Understatement of the century. When Zeke found out about the impending baby, nothing would keep him away. Time and circumstance would force Marcel to deal with a situation he didn't want to face. If this had happened ten or twenty years later, he'd have been fine with it. But right now? The timing couldn't have been worse. He was going to have to give up everything he'd ever wanted.

He turned away from the unused dining space and sank down on the sofa.

Holden rolled his eyes, and then he returned to the kitchen. Water ran, dishes clanked, and the dishwasher started up.

Marcel stared at the unwanted furniture, thinking about ways to rearrange everything to clear the space. The apartment wasn't small, but it wasn't large either. The space had been utilized well, but it hadn't been designed to include a practice space for a dancer. Underneath the apartment building, there was a parking garage. Was there storage space hiding even deeper underground?

And how was he going to tell Holden the reason he had to move out was because the second bedroom needed to be turned into a nursery? Holden wasn't a shifter, so this news was outside his realm of possibilities.

His thoughts were interrupted by something landing on his lap. Holden stood next to him, and Marcel looked down to find his phone sliding toward his crotch. The light blinked to indicate a notification. He unlocked it to find a message from Zeke. That's how he'd put his name into Marcel's phone, and the omega hadn't changed a thing.

Tag whatever you want gone. I'll send movers later today.

He scrolled up to find the original message. *I want to get rid of some of the furniture. How do I do that?*

Marcel scowled. "You texted Mr. Lowry on my phone."

"Well, I don't have his number."

"It was locked. How did you know my passcode?"

"It's your birthday, not the nuclear codes." Holden perched on the edge of the coffee table. "Look, I don't know why you're so upset. He's your contact person for the apartment and whatever else you need with regard to the accident."

Marcel had no intention of explaining why he was upset.

Holden sighed. "You said he wasn't a jerk."

"He's not." As much as Marcel wanted Mr. Lowry to have negative traits, he couldn't think of one thing wrong with the handsome alpha.

"Then I don't see the problem."

Marcel fell silent.

Shooting to his feet, Holden grabbed his dance bag. Rehearsals were even more intense as opening day approached. "You're an idiot. That guy is seriously hot. He has money, he seemed like a good guy, and he's into you. Everyone who saw you two together couldn't help but be smacked upside the head by the chemistry between you. I don't understand why you avoid him."

"If you think he's so wonderful, you go out with him." Self-loathing bombarded Marcel as he muttered the comeback. He couldn't stomach the idea of the father of his child with anyone else. He stifled a howl of objection from his inner canine.

"If I was gay, I would. Believe me—I'd even consider converting if he looked at me with half of the smolder in his eyes as he pointed in your direction. He barely noticed me or anyone else, Marcel. He only had eyes for you." Holden adjusted the strap on his bag and slipped into his street shoes. Before he left, he glanced over his shoulder. "Look, he said he was sending movers, okay? So you won't see him today either, not unless you want to."

The door closed behind Holden, and Marcel stared at his hands in his lap. He wanted to see Zeke—Mr. Lowry—with a need that left him weak and trembling. Closing his eyes, he steeled his nerves. This was exactly why he didn't need to get involved with an alpha. As much as having a child would derail his life, becoming an alpha's mate would wreak even more havoc with his life. He would cease to be anything except an omega—a househusband and father. His dreams wouldn't matter anymore—not even to himself.

Even thinking about living with Zeke—sharing his bed and his life—made Marcel begin to make deals and compromises. He'd done the same thing with law school, and look where that had landed him—depressed and in the emergency room because he'd tried to end it all.

He didn't want to travel that path again.

Rather than stay shut up in the apartment all day, Marcel went outside. The air had a bite to it, and occasional flurries turned somersaults in the downdrafts between buildings. When his hands were frozen through his gloves, he ducked into a coffee shop. As he sat down with a hot chocolate topped with whipped cream, his cell rang. The ringtone indicated his father, so he answered.

"Hi, Father. How are you?"

"It's winter, son. How about you come home?"

"This is my home, Father." Marcel closed his eyes and gritted his teeth. This wasn't the first time he'd discussed the issue with his father. Plus, the last thing he needed to do was to tell his father he had been knocked up by a handsome and charming dragon shifter. He tried to steer the conversation into neutral territory. "How are you doing?"

"I'm well. Business is brisk. We had a great third quarter, and this quarter is shaping up to be even better." Calvin Yardan's familiar baritone soothed Marcel as much as it put him on edge. "Dad misses you. It's been a month. At least come home for a visit. We'll send you money for the fare."

"I don't need money." He hadn't told his parents about the accident, but he had mentioned the apartment and the stipend. He might have let them assume it was coming from a job in the theater, which was a stupid move. Marcel's name was not listed in the cast, a fact his fathers wouldn't fail to notice if they looked up the show online.

If his fathers saw him, they'd immediately know the bump on his abdomen wasn't because he'd let himself go in the past month. They'd demand to know who was responsible, which was a tricky mess. Neither he nor Zeke had been operating on anything but instinct and primal need.

"Marcel, we worry about you." Aramond got on the line.

Marcel exhaled hard. If anyone could push his buttons, it was his dad. Of course, now that Marcel was going to be a dad himself, he had a lot of motivation to not cave to his dad's plea. "Don't, Dad. I'm fine."

"I'd feel a lot better if I knew where this stipend was coming from, Marcel."

Under no circumstances was he going to tell his parents he'd been in an accident. If he did that, both of them would be there, admonishing him for getting hurt, keeping secrets, and not holding out for a much larger settlement.

"Drop it, Dad."

"Older men prey upon naïve, young men like you."

Marcel gasped. Aramond had danced around the topic before, but he'd never come right out and accused Marcel of hooking up with a sugar daddy. "Dad, I'm not seeing anyone. I'm living with one of the other dancers. His parents, um, they give him an allowance."

It wasn't technically a lie. Holden's parents did give him money every month, but it wasn't much, and it wasn't close to covering the cost of a good-sized apartment in a nice, downtown neighborhood.

"Oh." Aramond's tone brightened. "Okay, then. That's awfully nice of Holden's parents. You be sure to write a thank-you note, okay? And maybe send a basket of baked goods, unless they're gluten-free people. Then send fruit or flowers."

"What about living expenses?" Calvin chimed in. "You need to eat, son."

"I eat, Father. Don't worry. I earn income. Maybe I'm not dancing, but I'm not sitting on my ass." Technically, he spent a lot of time sitting on his ass. Even while doing exercises, he had to avoid putting weight on his ankle. He wanted to yell that if they were so concerned, why hadn't they offered to help him out in his quest? His parents had plenty of money socked away for his education, but they refused to let him use it toward a career in the theater.

"If you change your mind and want to come home, just call," Calvin said. "Or if you want to enroll in Verdance School of Law, let us know. Or maybe something else—they have a great engineering program at Verdance University."

Of course they'd pay for them. If he consented to go back to school to get a degree they approved, they'd also pay for an apartment and food. Marcel wasn't going to let anyone control his life through the offer of food and shelter.

"I have to go Dad, Father. It was great to hear from you. Love you." He ended the call before they could say anything else he didn't want to hear.

Once upon a time, he'd been close with his parents. He missed those days.

Mired in dark thoughts, he nursed his chocolate and savored the whipped cream. When he finished, he headed to the trash bin near the door. By chance, he happened to glance across into the other half of the dining area. Somehow his gaze was drawn immediately to Zeke—Mr. Lowry. He shook his head, banishing the handsome man's first name from his mind in order to keep the alpha out of mental reach.

The sexy shifter sported a devilishly charming smile, and his eyes sparkled with mirth. He fished an ice cube from his beverage, and Marcel watched it disappear between those lush lips. He nodded as he chewed, and that's when Marcel noticed the man across from Zeke.

Like Zeke, he was tall. Where Zeke's light brown hair was close-shaved, this man had shoulder-length, white-blond hair. He possessed startling blue eyes, pale skin, and a delicate beauty. He grinned as he talked, his hands gesturing wildly as he described something.

It didn't take a genius to figure out what had happened. Zeke hadn't stopped by or contacted Marcel in over a month because he'd found another omega, this one a dragon shifter. He'd gone from insisting Marcel was meant to be his to romancing another omega.

Burning pain stabbed through Marcel's chest.

He wasn't jealous.

How could he possibly be jealous? He'd rejected Zeke's offer. He was pregnant with Zeke's child, not that Zeke knew anything along those lines.

Mesmerized by the horrific scene and his reaction to seeing Zeke, he touched his lips, remembering Zeke's searing kisses as he watched the alpha laugh and talk with another omega. His canine whined.

Zeke's head swung toward the sound, his enhanced senses finding the source with unerring accuracy. He acknowledged Marcel with a brief nod, and then his attention returned to his companion.

It was too much. Marcel shoved his empty cup into the trash and fled the coffee shop. To avoid walking past the window near Zeke, he took the long way home, circling the block to double back in the other direction.

The passage of several hours found him staring into the flames of a fire in his fireplace. Yeah, he was brooding. All told, this day had not been a good one. First, the phone call with his parents had been excruciating, and then seeing Zeke with another man had been more than Marcel could bear.

When a knock sounded on the door, he roused himself from the warmth and comfort of his emotional refuge to answer.

Zeke's broad shoulders filled the opening, his presence washing through Marcel's consciousness. It soothed his beast and sharpened the ache. No smile graced Zeke's handsome visage. "You wanted some furniture removed?"

"Yeah." Marcel noticed two men behind Zeke. He recognized James and Neven from the last time Mr. Lowry had visited the apartment. They'd brought food and toilet paper, all of which Marcel had appreciated. "The dining room set."

He led the trio down the short hall and into the apartment.

"I'm not sure how you're going to get the table out of here. The front hall is too narrow for it to fit." If today was the day for bad things to happen, then this was the third thing. Didn't that mean an end to his horrible day?

"You're on the ground floor," James said as he opened the slider to the porch. Neven picked up one end of the table, James grabbed the other, and together, they carried it outside.

Marcel searched for something to say. "I didn't expect you."

Rather than respond, Zeke lifted a chair in each hand and followed them outside and around the rear of the building. After a few minutes, the trio returned. James and Neven took the remaining four chairs, and Zeke regarded Marcel with a neutral expression. "You want the sideboard gone as well?"

"Yeah. I'm going to use the room as a studio, so I want it all gone."

Zeke opened and closed the doors and drawers. "You want the plates and silverware gone?"

Marcel had never looked in the drawers before. The kitchen came equipped with all that stuff. Why would anyone need more? "Please."

Without a word, Zeke disappeared. When he returned with his entourage, they had boxes and packing tape. In short order, the room was cleared. Even James and Neven had left, and now he was alone with Zeke.

The large alpha glanced around, his sharp gaze searching the space.

"Lose something?"

Zeke pressed his lips together, and vague hints of annoyance pinched his features, the first flicker of an emotion, and his gaze pointed over Marcel's shoulder. "You don't live alone."

"Holden moved in." He hadn't meant it as a challenge, but it came out that way.

Not a muscle twitched on the handsome shifter's face, confirming Marcel's worst fear—that Zeke had moved on with another omega.

Strange and intense feelings bombarded Marcel, all of them bad. He identified jealousy, fear, rage, and sadness. It was too much to contain. "I saw you with that omega." Though he tried to keep his tone neutral, it came out accusatory.

Now the alpha's penetrating gaze skewered Marcel. "Yes, you did."

"Are you telling him all the same lies you told me? I bet he's stupid enough to buy it." The green-eyed monster dictating his actions had turned Marcel into a man he didn't recognize. "As if you have an honest bone in your body. Whatever gets you laid, right?"

This was different from when he'd pushed Zeke before. Right now, he was out of control. Fueled by an irrational jumble of emotions, he had no idea what he was saying, but he knew he'd regret it later.

Zeke regarded him with steel lining his calm demeanor. "Tread lightly."

He might as well have told Marcel to calm down. It had the opposite effect. "Fuck that, and fuck you. I'm not afraid of you, Zeke. You come in here, playing like you're some big badass, when you're really just a glorified security guard."

The skin surrounding Zeke's lips went white because he pressed them together so hard. "I see you're still dedicated to being unreasonable. The dining room has been cleared as you requested, so I'll be going now."

He turned to leave, and at that moment, Marcel's canine whined. In response, an overwhelming rage—fueled by shame—had him leaping across the space to attack Zeke. It was the opposite of what he really wanted—the firm press of Zeke's lips against his, the gentle glide of his palm skating across Marcel's skin, the scrape of whiskers on his inner thigh as the alpha claimed every inch of his body. Instead, his frustrated fists flew, but they didn't connect. In short order, he found himself wrapped in Zeke's powerful arms, his back to the alpha's chest as the stronger man held him immobile.

"Let go of me. I fucking hate you." Really, Marcel hated himself, but thinking about the reasons behind the tumult of emotion hurt too much, and so he directed the feelings he couldn't handle at Zeke.

A bark of strangled laughter shot from Zeke. "That's rich. You hate me because I refuse to stay and suffer your abuse."

Marcel struggled, fighting Zeke's hold, but the alpha's arms were like iron bands.

"This isn't a cease-fire, cupcake, but if you stop fighting and agree not to attack me again, I'll let you go, and then I'll leave peacefully."

Though the idea of Zeke leaving filled him with a sadness that crushed his chest, Marcel forced his body to relax. He sagged against the alpha, and Zeke's hold softened. Before he knew what he was doing, Marcel turned in Zeke's arms and tilted his face up. Subsonic whines escaped from his throat, and his hands slid over the alpha's biceps to grasp at his shoulders.

"Zeke." The name, the one he'd been withholding to keep emotional distance between them, floated out on a desperate exhalation.

The alpha heeded his plea. Zeke didn't bother with a gentle teasing. He closed his lips over Marcel's devouring him with unrestrained passion. Marcel responded in kind. He opened to the alpha—*his alpha*—and melted against the body of the man he'd wanted since the moment he walked into that hospital room looking like a sexy god in a three-piece suit.

The kiss heated Marcel from the inside, sparking a blaze that had been smoldering for a month. It drugged him, creating a sharp need while leaving his limbs too heavy to move.

Suddenly Zeke broke the kiss and pushed Marcel away. Stunned, Marcel took a moment to process what was happening. The whites of Zeke's eyes had turned black, and his dark pupils had become vertical slits. The blue irises were still there, though that hint of color only emphasized the darkness surrounding it. The tip of a forked tongue flickered out to whet Zeke's lower lip.

The danger of this apex predator was readily apparent, but Marcel could find nothing that inspired fear. If anything, Zeke's appearance promised a passionate encounter.

"Please don't stop," Marcel breathed. He'd never begged in his life, but he'd do it now because that one taste already haunted him.

"You hate me," Zeke reminded him. "If I get you pregnant, you'll hate me even more."

"Wear a condom." Where had that come from? It was already too late.

"No."

It didn't matter. The deed was done. "Fine. No condom. Fuck me anyway."

Zeke might have been surprised, but his only discernible expression was raw and undisguised need. "You're sure?"

"Yes. I'm sure." Marcel lifted his shirt over his head and peeled out of his sweats. He stood unsteadily, not because his ankle was bothering him, but because his body trembled with anticipation.

The alpha's gaze roved Marcel's form, drinking in the visual like an elixir. If he noticed Marcel's rounded belly or understood what it meant, then he didn't comment. He toed off his shoes and tossed his jacket over the arm of the sofa. In a blur of movement, Zeke scooped Marcel in his arms and carried him to the bedroom. He set Marcel on the bed and settled his weight on top of him.

Marcel spread his legs and wrapped his arms around Zeke's neck. "Kiss me, Zeke." Saying the alpha's name like a caress, Marcel assumed control. He smiled as Zeke's lips brushed against his, but the moment Zeke's tongue plundered his mouth, he understood Zeke was the one in control. Marcel might not be a submissive omega, but Zeke was a dominant alpha. He didn't do things by half measures.

Zeke kissed like a god, staking his claim and taking his due while he left behind sweet bliss. This time when he broke off the kiss, his mouth explored Marcel's chin and the line of his jaw with the scrape of his teeth and nips from his strong lips. That drugged feeling returned, but this time Marcel's limbs didn't feel heavy. Tingles of electricity shot through his synapses, making him writhe.

Marcel wanted to be even closer to Zeke. He arched and undulated, caressing the alpha with grasping strokes and wayward scratches. He tried to undress his lover, but his fingers were all thumbs, and he fumbled the buttons. Mindless with need, he whimpered and moaned as Zeke explored his body.

"Naked," he begged.

If Zeke heard the plea, he ignored it. His mouth traveled a leisurely path down Marcel's chest in a series of light bites and barely-there licks. Those strong hands moved over his skin, gently stoking the frenzy. He lifted Marcel, and then the last garment—white boxer briefs—was gone.

Kneeling up, Zeke held Marcel in place with the power of his gaze. It moved across Marcel's body, reactivating the effect of every single kiss, bite, and caress simultaneously. Marcel struggled not to climax.

Zeke loosened his tie, and then he worked the buttons on his shirt and vest. "Touch yourself, Marcel. I want to see you work that magnificent cock."

His cock was the single place Zeke hadn't yet explored. As much as Marcel wanted his alpha to touch him, he knew better than to argue. Now was not the time to drive Zeke over the edge, not with the lizardlike slits his eyes had become. The element of inherent danger made Marcel's cock even harder.

He fisted his cock. "Do you want to see me come?"

Zeke's tongue darted out. It was long and thin, with a forked tip that gave his words a sexy sibilance. "Yes."

The buttons on his shirt open, Zeke shrugged out of it. He tossed the vest, shirt, and tie to the chair beside the bed. Then he rose to his knees to tackle his belt and pants. Marcel watched eagerly as Zeke revealed the actual size of the impressive member he'd felt when the alpha had held him against his body. Last time had been too quick, too frenzied for him to have paid much attention to details, and his animal side only recalled feelings, impressions, and sensations.

As was true of the rest of him, Zeke's dick was extra large. The long, thick shaft was ribbed, and a single pearl of wetness spilled from the purpled crown. Unable to control himself, Marcel sat up and stole it with a single lick. It tasted heavenly, and he couldn't stop with a mere sample. Wrapping his hand around Zeke's cock, he wet the tip and closed his mouth over the smooth head.

Zeke held still as Marcel moaned around his cock. He licked the length, the musky, salty flavor causing him to salivate for even more of a taste. Not nearly enough time passed before Zeke grasped Marcel's head and forced him to abandon his ministrations.

He whined, a subsonic noise that the alpha clearly heard.

With an arrogant grin, Zeke pushed Marcel back and pinned him to the bed. "Cease your whining, cupcake. I'm not going to come in your mouth—this time."

The whining wasn't something he could control. It came from his shifter side, a primal force that wouldn't be denied. But something about being pinned by his alpha calmed the frenzy because it promised to sate the lingering ache.

Zeke lifted Marcel's legs out of the way, and he positioned his wet cock at Marcel's sphincter. "Inhale, omega. This won't hurt unless I want it to."

With that ominous assurance, Marcel filled his lungs.

"Now let it out slowly."

As he did, Zeke pressed forward. The bulbous crown stretched his opening. Though it was impossibly large, it didn't hurt. The exhalation came harder as each ridge impaled him anew, and by the time Zeke was all the way inside, Marcel gasped for air.

Had Zeke taken this kind of care last time? In the blur of memory from that night, Marcel could recall tender touches and the bliss of having Zeke inside him.

"Breathe, Marcel. That's it. Relax, cupcake. I'm going to make you feel so good, you'll have plenty of reasons to forget why you hate me."

"Don't hate you." Marcel wrapped his legs around Zeke's waist and grasped the alpha's arms for an anchor. "Want you. Need you. Dream about you."

These were confessions Marcel hadn't meant to make, but he couldn't seem to stop the confessional flow. He was grateful when Zeke's mouth claimed his. Holding his weight on his elbows, the alpha rocked into Marcel, and his tongue swept into Marcel's mouth. Zeke claimed every part of the omega.

His pace increased, and he fucked Marcel faster, swiveling his hips in a sinful way that elicited frantic cries from Marcel's depths. Then his hand closed over Marcel's, ripping it from where he grasped Zeke's shoulder, and he guided it between their bodies.

"Touch yourself, Marcel. I want to see you climax."

It wouldn't take much to get him there. Passion roared through Marcel's body, and touching his cock made every cell in his body explode with the force of his orgasm. His ejaculate shot out, streams coating his stomach and splashing onto Zeke's chest.

Without missing a beat, the alpha bent his head down, and that long tongue snaked out, slurping up every drop. Incredibly enough, the distraction didn't interrupt Zeke's rhythm. His hips moved faster and faster. The cords on his neck stood out. Very soon, he threw back his head and roared. Flames shot from his mouth as his orgasm emptied into Marcel's body.

His body shuddered as the last drops wrung from him, and then Zeke collapsed on top of Marcel.

Trembling with the aftershocks, Marcel clung to the alpha he'd rejected. As their bodies cooled, Marcel thought about what it would be like to have Zeke like this all the time. Would he eventually forget he'd ever dreamed of dancing under the spotlight? Could this be enough to keep Marcel from the depths of the abyss that had taken hold of him not so very long ago?

Zeke gently extracted his cock. He pressed a kiss to the hollow of Marcel's throat, and then he went into the bathroom to clean up.

Everything—from the first kiss to the last—had been both hot and romantic. Zeke hadn't tempered his passion or hidden his emotions. The alpha was all-in. Marcel had only to accept what he offered.

A small part of him wanted that, but the rest of him vehemently rebelled. Against what, he wasn't sure. In a little over a month, he would have a baby to care for. Did he want to do that by himself, did he want to give it to Zeke to raise, or did he want to wave farewell to the dream of who he wanted to be?

On the verge of tears, he snatched up his underwear from the floor and slid into it.

Zeke returned. He stood in the doorway, a magnificent specimen that rivaled anything carved in marble, his head cocked to the side as he assessed the situation. "You've decided to hate me again."

"No." Marcel had never hated Zeke. He hated himself for his weakness. "You should get dressed and go home. Holden will be back soon."

Danger signs blazed in Zeke's eyes, but Marcel chose to ignore them. He took one long stride into the room. "I won't play games with you, Marcel. You belong to me."

"You have an omega. I saw you with him."

"He is not mine." Zeke snatched him up, iron bands around his arms holding him so that only his toes touched the floor. "You are mine, and I am yours." What began as a violent claim ended with a frantic offering.

"Yeah, right," Marcel scoffed. He called on the ugliness that came with his self-loathing, and he turned it on Zeke. "You made it pretty clear from the start that you wanted to have sex with me. Maybe I just wanted to keep a roof over my head. Hey — if I keep letting you fuck me, can I stay here for longer than six months?"

That dangerous light turned ominous. "You can stay here for as long as you fucking want. But I won't let you debase what is between us by taking other lovers. Holden moves out today."

Marcel knew full well what Zeke thought, though he was a little puzzled that the alpha couldn't figure out that they were just friends. Surely he could tell by scent alone Marcel hadn't even entertained the thought of being with another man since the moment he laid eyes on his alpha — even though he'd rejected Zeke's claim.

And yet Marcel sought to play a dangerous game. "Holden is not moving out. You don't get to dictate who lives here. That's not in the settlement."

With stiff movements, Zeke dressed.

Recognizing that he'd gone too far — he didn't mind pissing Zeke off, but he ached to see he'd hurt the alpha — Marcel went to him. He set his palms against Zeke's bare chest, barring him from buttoning his shirt. "He's not my lover. We're just friends. You know that."

Zeke froze. His gaze zeroed in on Marcel's briefs. "I'm not stupid, Marcel. His scent is all over you."

The pain hiding behind Zeke's blue eyes and the stiffness of his shoulders skewered Marcel. He rested his hands on Zeke's cheeks, seeking to soothe his alpha's torment. "I swear he's not. Holden is straight. We're just friends. I let him stay in the second bedroom, and he helps me out with the things I can't do." Then he realized the problem. The alpha shifter could smell everything in the apartment. "These are his underwear, yes. It's laundry day, and I only have the clothes I brought in my backpack. He lent me the sweats and shirt I was wearing earlier."

Holden was larger than Marcel, and the tight shirts and leotards Marcel had packed didn't work well with his increased midsection. He needed paternity clothes.

Disbelief temporarily replaced the pain. "You're wearing another man's underwear? The stipend is enough for you to buy your own."

There had been expenses first month that ate up the stipend — fees to set up various services, purchases related to his injuries, and the cost of transportation since he couldn't make it to the bus stop. That heavenly sweet potato mash he craved. Knowing any explanation would be inadequate in the face of Zeke's upset, Marcel shrugged. "I spent it all."

Zeke's frown said enough. He disapproved of Marcel's actions, and he was going to admonish Marcel for not calling him to ask for what he needed.

This was going in a direction Marcel didn't care to travel. He scrambled for footing. "Look, I'm not sleeping with other guys, okay? But that doesn't mean we're together. This was a one-off. Or, a two-off. You were an itch I had to scratch, and now it's over."

That harsh gaze impaled Marcel with icicles. Zeke severed contact, pushing Marcel back. "You want to reject your omega nature and my claim on you as your alpha. I can't—and won't—force you into a relationship you don't want. But I won't pretend what you did today is okay. You used me. You used my need to love and protect you against me, and I will never forget the depths to which your treacherous heart will sink to get what you want."

For the first time in his life, Marcel didn't know what to say. His actions didn't have anything to do with Zeke. They were the actions of a man who was desperate not to lose everything that made him who he was—and yet, he remained doomed. This wasn't something a dragon alpha would understand. He knew from his budding friendship with Edgar what he'd have to give up. Edgar served his dragon alpha as a husband and father. He was everything an alpha from an ancient race expected from an omega.

Marcel knew he wasn't cut out for that life. He'd never be what Zeke wanted him to be, and that fact stabbed at his heart, taunting him with what he could never have—an alpha who respected him and who supported his dreams. It had been easier to accept he'd always be alone when he hadn't met an alpha who invaded his every thought and made his canine cry with wanting. But now it was different. Now it hurt.

He wanted to argue with Zeke, but he had nothing substantive to say that would sway the alpha. Any reason he gave would only induce Zeke to argue against him, especially if he admitted he was pregnant. Marcel sat heavily on the bed, his gaze as sullen and dark as his thoughts.

Zeke left the room. When he returned a few minutes later, he was fully dressed. He extracted his wallet from his inside breast pocket and opened it up. He pulled out a wad of cash and tossed it to the bed. The stack of bills hit the mussed cover and scattered. "That should be enough for underwear of your own and some new clothes."

Then he was gone. The apartment was noticeably colder and lonelier.

Marcel glanced at the cash, automatically counting the five hundred in various bills. He wondered if Zeke's goal had been to make him feel as used as he'd made Zeke feel. If so, mission accomplished.

A single tear slipped down his cheek, and then a torrent followed.

Chapter 7

Zeke

Claiming his omega should have been a momentous occasion. Though it was their second coupling, the first had been driven by primal instinct. This time had been different. Passion and need had guided them, not forces beyond their control.

Given Marcel's less-than-enthusiastic reaction to Zeke's initial offer, he hadn't expected his omega to turn into a pussy cat. But he had expected Marcel's attitude to change.

Maybe he wouldn't come completely around, but he should have been at least open to seeing Zeke again.

Instead, he'd reiterated that Zeke had no place in his life.

An empty house was not where Zeke wanted to be, so when he left Marcel's place, he headed down the street. In a haze of misery that echoed with the beat of a false heart, he walked aimlessly. Drizzle fell from the clouds, an icy mixture that mirrored his feelings. A little while later, a sign on a window for drink specials caught his attention.

Alcohol would dull the pain.

He went into Petrichor and sat at the bar, his gaze downcast because he didn't want to engage in conversation. His cash was gone, so he slapped a credit card on the counter.

That got the barkeep's attention. "You want to run a tab?"

"Yes. Four shots of tequila. Keep them coming."

"Zeke?" Another barkeep appeared when the first had gone to fill his order.

Zeke looked up to find Chay staring at him. Chayton Sadler was Koren's omega. Chay hadn't been looking for a relationship, but he hadn't fought his instincts, and he hadn't rejected the love and devotion Koren offered. The pair had twin boys who were about six months old. They were blissfully happy.

Zeke wanted that with Marcel. He wanted it so badly, but the desire tasted bitter in his throat.

"Chay? I didn't know you worked here." He hadn't known Chay worked at all. He'd wanted to be a stay-at-home dad.

He grinned, a hint of mischief lighting his brown eyes. "I help out every now and again. I end up working about one or two evenings a week. It's nice to get out of the house and do my own thing." He leaned closer. "And it gives Koren time alone with the boys. I'm sure I'll come home to a mess, but they'll have had fun, and that's the important thing."

Zeke reflected on Marcel's assertion that he wouldn't let him work. In reality, he'd encourage Marcel to do anything that made him happy. He'd support Marcel's dreams.

The barkeeper returned with the shots, and Zeke downed them in quick succession. Those were replaced immediately, and Zeke made short work of round two.

Chay's eyes widened. "Want to talk about it?"

Turning the last shot upside down, he grunted. "My omega is a dick."

Wincing, Chay waved away the bartender who'd returned with two more shots. "That's harsh."

"It's harsh that you won't let me drink." He whistled for the bartender to come back. "Ignore this one. Keep them coming. When I pass out, Chay can call someone to cart my sorry ass home."

Zeke downed another shot, and when he reached for his tenth, Chay slapped his hand over the glass. "Why is your omega being a dick?"

Alcohol took a while to have an effect on him. Not only was he a large man, but his shifter blood filtered out the effects faster than normal. If he wanted to get wasted, he had to drink a lot of booze very quickly. Right now, he was pleasantly buzzed. That, combined with Chay's sweet manner, made him more amenable to a conversation he didn't want to have.

"He's being a dick because he doesn't want to be my omega. He thinks I'm going to make him give up his career to take care of me and our children."

"Did you tell him that's what you wanted?" Chay's expression remained sympathetic.

"No. He came out of nowhere with that accusation." Zeke picked up one of the shot glasses that didn't have Chay's hand over it, and he downed the contents. "I was nice to him. I gave him everything he asked for."

"You're talking about the settlement." Chay removed the empty glasses, leaving Zeke with two.

"Yeah." Zeke smiled at the memory of the first time he'd set eyes on Marcel. "He could have asked for so much more, and he knew it. But he only wanted what he needed to make it through to the next audition. I thought he was principled. I liked that about him."

He followed with another shot.

Chay set a glass of water between them on the bar.

Zeke rejected it out of hand, the same way Marcel had rejected him.

"We both felt it." He rubbed a hand over his eyes, willing away the bleariness. "I was nice to him, and he rejected me. With every look, word, and action, he told me to stay away. So I did. Until he texted me."

Chay nudged the water closer. "What did he text you?"

Zeke downed another shot. "Said he wanted furniture moved."

He heard the slur in his words, but he only cared that his chest ached a little less.

"Did you move the furniture? Is that where you were this afternoon?"

"Yeah. He wants to dance in the dining room. We took out the table and stuff. Then he kissed me. We had sex, and then he kicked me out. He was wearing another man's underwear." He drank the last shot. "Just friends, my ass. Four more."

Chay didn't appear thrilled, but he poured four more shots of tequila, and he lined them up in front of Zeke. "Go slow. If you pass out, you'll fall down and crack your thick skull open."

"Marcel is the one with the thick skull. I think I'm the one with thin skin." He barely knew the man, so why did his constant rejection hurt so fucking much?

"Alphas need love too. You're all big and tough on the outside, but inside, you're made of marshmallow fluff." Chay closed his hand over Zeke's fist. "Did he cheat on you?"

In order to cheat, there needed to be a relationship. Even so, Marcel had insisted he hadn't been with another man. "I don't fucking know."

Zeke rubbed his eyes harder. Something nagged at him, a sense he'd noted something without noticing it.

"Hey, be careful." Chay's soft touch urged his hand away from his face. "You're popping out a talon, there. You might scratch your eye out."

By way of response, Zeke snatched up another shot and downed it. His throat must have been numb because it didn't burn. At least something on him was immune to pain.

"So, to sum up — your omega doesn't want to be in a relationship with you because he thinks you're going to make him give up his dancing career?"

"Every time I see him, he acts like a complete asshole. He says mean things, and then he kisses me, and then he says more mean things. How can my dragon want to be with someone like that?" He drank another shot because his brain was still working too well.

"You liked him when you first met him, and Edgar said he was nice."

Zeke snorted. "What the fuck does Edgar know? He likes everyone, and everyone likes him. Even Tito likes him, and Tito hates everyone who isn't one of us." He drank two shots for punctuation.

Chay took away the empty glasses and replaced them with four more. Koren had a good omega on his hands, one who knew when to stop arguing and give an alpha what he needed. Leaning on his elbows, Chay said, "Edgar isn't a pushover. You're family to him, and that means he's going to be loyal to you no matter what. For that matter, I'm the same way. Dog people are like that."

Blinking as he processed what Chay was trying to tell him, Zeke froze for a few moments. Then he snorted. "Poodles must be the assholes of the canine community."

"They're high-maintenance, they like a quiet and orderly environment, and they don't react well when things don't go the way they expect. He needs time to acclimate to your presence in his life."

Zeke had been abiding by Marcel's wish for him to stay away. "I don't have a presence in his life."

"We'll work on changing that." Chay grinned, but it was directed over Zeke's shoulder.

Turning to find who merited a friendly greeting from his friend's omega, Zeke saw Amaricio behind him. "Grange?" He leveled an accusation at Chay. "You weren't supposed to call Amar until I passed out."

"You're not going to pass out. I've been giving you mostly water with a hint of tequila in shot glasses. You'll thank me in the morning." Chay snagged his hand. "Don't be discouraged. He may be acting like a jerk, but I think he's just terrified. Someone has hurt your omega, my friend, and he's determined to not let it happen again. You're going to have to figure out how to make him trust you."

Zeke rose on wobbly legs. Amar's arm came around his waist. "Come on, buddy. Let's get you home."

His empty and lonely home was where he had lots of alcohol and no busybody omega to stop him from drinking it all. He went willingly.

Only Granger didn't take him home. Zeke realized that in the elevator. His three-story brownstone didn't have an elevator. "Hey—this is your building."

"It is."

The door to Granger's apartment opened just after the elevator let them off. Edgar, Amar's devoted omega, stood there with his arms crossed and a sour expression on his face.

"Fuck," Zeke said. "We woke up the babies."

Edgar let loose a long-suffering sigh and rolled his eyes. "The babies are not yet asleep. It's only seven o'clock. It is, however, much too early for you to be fall-down drunk."

"I have a good reason." Zeke meant to say that, but the convoluted slur that came out of his mouth didn't match the intention.

Edgar opened the door wider. "Normally I wouldn't let you around the kids in this state, but I think they're too young to notice. They toddle around and fall down as well."

"I haven't fallen," Zeke mumbled.

"That's because I'm pretty much carrying you," Grange supplied.

"I don't want to be here." Zeke surveyed the wreck of the living room, noting the three small persons running around wearing nothing but diapers. They yelled to one another in their unique, babbling language, and the mess of toys made the idea of navigating the room problematic, at best.

"Tough shit," Granger said. "I'm not leaving you alone when you're like this, and Edgar needs help bathing the triplets."

He blinked at his buddy. "You want a drunk guy to bathe your kids? I know nothing about kids, but that seems irresponsible."

Edgar pointed to the sofa near the fireplace. "Put him there. I'll make coffee."

Zeke lurched forward, his first try at walking without support. "If you call me a cab, I'll go home. I'm not fit company right now."

"Sit down, Zeke. You'll drink coffee, and Amar will make up the sofa bed in his office." Edgar gave the order as he disappeared into the kitchen.

Peering at Granger, Zeke chuckled. "Who's the boss around here?"

"You'll learn soon enough not to argue with an omega in caretaker mode. Besides, he's only making sure you're okay, which is what I want. The orders might come from him, but he's following my wishes."

For the next hour, Zeke sat in the assigned chair, ignored the coffee, and listened to his friends put their children to bed. And he yearned for a similar bliss.

Morning found him in the same chair. He opened his eyes to find sunlight streaking through the tall windows. It didn't hurt his head as much as he'd expected. Someone had thrown a blanket over him and reclined the chair so that he didn't get a crick in his neck. They'd also removed his shoes and loosened his tie. Slowly he got to his feet, careful to avoid the stray toys that still littered the floor.

He freshened up in the bathroom. He was going to need to swing by his place to shower and change, but by the time he emerged, he was satisfied he didn't look too much like he'd endured a rough night.

His nose took him to the kitchen, where he found Edgar hovering over delicious smells sizzling on the stove. Edgar smiled as Zeke entered his domain. "Good morning. Coffee is in the pot, and breakfast will be done in about ten minutes."

Zeke's stomach rumbled. "I don't want to interrupt your morning. I'll grab something at the bakery on my way to work."

Edgar paused to level a firm look at Zeke. The blond patch over his eye ruined the effect. Rather than stern, he merely looked cute. "Ezekiel Lowry, you are not interrupting my morning. Pour yourself a mug of coffee, and tell me about all your troubles. I'm good at relationships."

His sixth sense gave him a sinking feeling. "Chay already told you everything." He was sure Chay had told everyone by now.

"He said Marcel isn't playing nice." Edgar spooned scrambled eggs onto a plate and added six sausage links to it. He set it in front of Zeke. "Is it a waste of time to give you fruit?"

"Yes." Zeke liked fruit, just not for breakfast. It was a snack food. "Thank you. It smells great."

Edgar set his hand on Zeke's shoulder. "For what it's worth, I agree with Chay. I think he's reacting out of fear."

He speared a sausage link. "I don't know how to work with that. I've been charming, serious, funny, noncommittal, and angry. So far, he seems to like pushing my buttons and leading me on."

"I don't think he's leading you on." Edgar returned to the stove. "He's fighting his omega nature, and that's like trying to live your life as someone you're not. It kills you from the inside."

"What kills you from the inside?" Granger joined them. He planted a kiss on Edgar's cheek and took the plate his omega handed to him.

"Not being true to yourself."

Grange sat down and dug into his breakfast. "I take it you're referring to Marcel?"

"Yes. The rest of us are enlightened." Edgar sat down last. On his plate, he had less meat, but he'd included orange slices. "You need a plan. Kill him with kindness."

"I tried being nice. He just turns into more of a dick."

"That means you're getting through to him." Edgar pronounced his conclusion with a grin.

Zeke's plate was clear, and so was his head. He sat back and sipped his coffee. "Edgar, I'm not going to play games with him, and we're not going to solve this in one morning. Thank you for breakfast and for your friendship. It means a lot to have the two of you on my side."

He stood.

Granger watched him closely. "Are you going to work?"

"I have to take Anshu to meet a Silver-Wing in Miami, so I probably won't be in the office today." With that, a toddler called out, and Zeke quietly excused himself.

The elevator opened on the ground floor, and Zeke couldn't stop from thinking about Marcel as he exited. Less than a hundred yards away, his omega was probably asleep. The idea of Marcel, untroubled by what had happened between them, blissfully sleeping, bothered him. He wanted the omega to suffer for his actions the same way he was torturing Zeke. It wasn't fair.

Life wasn't fair, he knew, but that didn't mean he would ever stop looking for things to work out in his favor.

With that thought in mind, he focused on the things he needed to do in order to accomplish everything on his agenda. First on the list was the need to shower. Then he needed to pick up Anshu, and there was no way they'd make it to the airport on time. He needed to delay the flight, and the ripple effect was going to mess up his plan for the whole day.

He slid his phone from his pocket and scrolled through his contacts.

"Zeke?"

His dragon recognized Marcel's voice before it registered in his consciousness. Mid-stride, Zeke paused. He lifted a brow at the omega, but he said nothing.

Heat darkened Marcel's cheeks, giving them a hint of redness under his ebony skin. "I, um, I..." He gestured behind Zeke, in the general direction of his apartment. "Do you have a couple of minutes? I wanted to talk to you."

Bruised and still licking his wounds from his last encounter with Marcel, Zeke resumed walking. "I don't. If you need something, call my office. Someone there will take care of whatever you need."

He dialed Tito. As the phone rang, he slid into the backseat of the car he'd called to pick him up. The opposite door opened, and Marcel got in. Zeke watched him for a moment, curious as to what new game Marcel had decided to play.

Then Tito answered, and he decided to ignore his unexpected guest.

"Ezekiel. What's wrong?" Tito got right to the point. The time when Zeke might call his mentor for a social chat had passed.

"I'm running late. Can you pick up Anshu and bring him to my place?"

"Your flight leaves in an hour."

"Two hours. I can make it." He might not be able to make it, but he was sure as hell going to try. In the past month, he'd spent a lot of time brokering meetings between Anshu Bray, the last living dragon omega, and alphas from various tribes. He'd attempted to find a Sharp-Winged companion, but no alphas had clicked with Anshu. And, now that Zeke knew what it meant to find his omega, he wouldn't let Anshu settle for anything less than the man he was meant to be with.

"With my help." Smugness mixed with a hint of relief in Tito's tone.

"Yes. Or I can call someone else, if you're busy."

While Anshu could call a ride and get himself to Zeke's house—or to the airport—Zeke felt responsible for the omega he'd recently begun to think of as a friend. He'd prefer Anshu not have to do any of those things for himself.

It wasn't that Zeke wanted Anshu for himself—now that he'd met Marcel, only that omega could complete him—but he wanted to show the omega the respect he deserved and what he should expect from his eventual mate.

"I'll do it," Tito said. "Be ready in thirty minutes."

Next, he called his administrative assistant to go over a list of tasks that needed to be completed before the end of the day. Just because he wasn't going to be in the office didn't mean deadlines had moved.

Before he finished, the taxi pulled up in front of his three-story brownstone. It was in an older section of the city, and it had belonged to Tito at one time. When Zeke had moved to Verdance, he'd fallen in love with the place, and Tito had sold it to him at a steep discount.

He paid the driver using an app, and when he got out of the car, Marcel did the same. Wordlessly, the omega followed him to the front door. Though Zeke didn't pay direct attention to Marcel, he was hyperaware of the omega.

When he finished with his admin, he called Anshu to inform him of the change in plans. Marcel followed him into the house, but when he loosened his tie and mounted the stairs, Marcel remained on the first level.

It was just as well. Zeke wasn't sure how long he could maintain the façade of nonchalance without the armor of his clothes. He showered, the process taking a little longer because he kept picturing his omega in there with him. Afterward he shaved.

The front bell rang as he finished up. He shoved his legs into pants and flew down two flights of stairs. Marcel hovered at the opening between the living room and hallway. Fleetingly, Zeke wondered if the omega had taken the time to explore the house. It had a lot of space, plenty of room to raise a family.

And if Marcel wanted, Zeke could convert the basement into a dance studio. It had high enough ceilings.

He shook all that away as he opened the door. Anshu waited on the small porch with Tito behind him. Though this was the tenth meeting in two weeks, he'd dressed to impress.

"Good morning." He gestured for Anshu to come inside. To Tito, he said, "Thanks for bringing him. I'll take it from here."

Tito pushed past Zeke and into the foyer. "I've decided to accompany you. It's been a while since we've spent time together, and I haven't been to Miami in years."

Though Zeke wanted to refuse Tito, he refrained. Tito was his boss, the unofficial head of the Sharp-Winged tribe, and more than that, a huge part of him missed the man who'd been so vitally important to him for so many years.

Amaricio hadn't forgiven Tito for kidnapping Edgar, which meant the rest of them were also not friendly with the elder dragon, but he knew Tito wouldn't go against the High Council's edicts. Seeing Anshu safely mated would be a coup for the Sharp-Winged Tribe, and since Anshu was one of the two scientists intent on studying the issue of the critically endangered omegas, it could only add insight into the dying off of the dragon species.

"Sure. Give me a minute to get dressed, and we'll be on our way." He headed up the stairs.

As he'd expected, Tito followed him. On the second floor, he said, "Ezekiel, is that a canine omega in your living room?"

"Yes."

"He's yours?"

"No." The honest answer ripped into his battered heart. "But you'll leave him be."

Marcel

The plane lifted into the air, and Marcel yawned to adjust his ears to the changing pressure. When he'd tossed and turned the night before, imagining the hoops he'd have to jump through in order to talk to Zeke again, he hadn't envisioned anything remotely like the situation in which he now found himself.

Hurting Zeke had never been in his master plan. In a perfect world, he could have his alpha and his career. But this world was far from perfect, and experience had taught him that he'd never get anywhere if he didn't pursue his dreams with a single-minded focus.

The way Zeke had left haunted him.

Scenes of the money skittering across the bed.

The hard, remote look in Zeke's eyes.

A tortured acceptance that Marcel would never belong to him.

The anger underneath it all.

He washed a hand over his eyes, an ineffectual move that did not blot out the knowledge he'd done some serious damage to an innocent man.

This morning, his heart had raced when he'd spotted Zeke in his building. He'd briefly nursed a hope the alpha was there because he'd bounced back. More than anything, Marcel wanted Zeke to be okay. The way Zeke had dismissed him had stung, a small retaliation considering what Marcel had done to the alpha.

Hopping into that car had been a bold move, uncharacteristic of a man who planned out every second of his day. As the private plane leveled off, he accepted the fact that his color-coded schedule was blown.

Fluttering in his abdomen took his breath away, and he closed his eyes as joy and sadness washed over him. He couldn't do this alone, and he dreaded giving up either the baby or his dreams, but one of them had to go.

He wondered at the way Zeke ignored him. The alpha didn't once look his way or speak to him, but he was consistently aware of Marcel's location and needs. He'd taken care of adding Marcel to the flight manifest without a word. He opened doors and made sure Marcel didn't fall too far behind the group. He'd even bought him a snack in the airport, absently handing the pastry to Marcel as he herded Anshu toward the concourse.

Marcel chose a seat that wasn't in the grouping with the other three passengers. He sat on a sofa toward the front of the cabin. It afforded him a way to watch Zeke and the others, and it allowed them privacy to discuss the business reasons behind the trip. Marcel wasn't sure where they were going, but he was reassured by the fact that none of them had brought an overnight bag.

Zeke and Tito occupied wide, comfortable chairs, and Anshu—the omega he'd seen with Zeke in the coffee shop—sat across from them. The trio were definitely dragon shifters, and they were very different from the smaller shifters Marcel had known growing up.

For starters, they were all very tall and muscular. Even Anshu, who was thin and pale in comparison, sported a formidable and enviable build. He wore stylish clothes that set off his blue eyes, and he'd tied his white-blond hair back in a sleek ponytail.

Tito was handsome for an older man, and Marcel sensed the tension between him and Zeke.

And Zeke—he was the epitome of leading-man handsome. The scruffy beard and the tired smudges under his eyes had disappeared with a shower. The dress shirt he wore hugged his shoulders and fit snugly over his massive biceps. His eyes didn't shine, not even when he smiled at something Anshu said.

He did not smile at Tito. It seemed the older shifter was on Zeke's shit list along with Marcel. He wondered what had happened to land him there. If he was being fair, Zeke had given Marcel a lot of chances before he'd become withdrawn and remote, and so he figured Tito must have really fucked up as well.

The three of them conversed in low tones. Marcel overheard snatches, enough to figure out they were taking Anshu to meet a potential alpha. Marcel wondered if Zeke might have tried for the attractive omega's hand if his dragon hadn't purred for Marcel.

He also wondered if his canine would ever stop whining for another taste of Zeke's dizzying kisses or the touch of his hands all over Marcel's body.

The seatbelt light went off, and Marcel got up onto his knees to look out the window. He hadn't set out to fuck up his life, but that's exactly what he'd done. The next time someone mugged him, he was going to let them take his stuff. Fighting for material possessions hadn't turned out so well for him.

"We haven't been properly introduced."

Marcel jumped. He'd been too absorbed in his dark thoughts to notice Anshu's approach. Disconcerted, he fumbled for a reply. "I know who you are."

"And I know who you are." Anshu grinned. "But that doesn't mean we've been introduced." He stuck out a hand. "Anshu Bray, scientist extraordinaire for Gliding Principles. I'm currently on loan to Draco International. I'm working with Koren Tafari on a genetics project."

After that detailed introduction, Marcel chuckled. "Marcel Yardan, aspiring dancer. I was cast in *Dance of the Dragons* at the Verdance Theater until an unfortunate accident left me injured, and I lost my job." He held up his right arm, still in a cast, and then he pointed to his ankle, which was wrapped tight. "If I'd known I was going to be gone this long, I would have brought my crutches. I'm good for short distances only at this point."

Anshu nodded. "I heard about the mix-up with Zane. I hope you're not too mad at him. He's a good guy. It was an honest mistake."

Honestly, Marcel hadn't thought about Zane Velan in a long time. He'd been too focused on the problems that had come after. "I'm not angry with him. He was a victim, too." Abandoning the window, he sat next to Anshu.

Motioning toward the alphas who had their heads together and conversed in low tones, Anshu said, "I take it you and Zeke had a disagreement?"

"You could say that."

Anshu lowered his voice and leaned closer to Marcel. "Mind if I stick my nose into your business and ask about it?"

Marcel's first reaction was to wonder about Anshu's motive. "Why do you care?"

He lifted a shoulder. "I've known Zeke, from a distance, my whole life. We come from rival tribes, and we've had our share of conflict. He doesn't have to help me find an alpha—a task my own tribe has all but abandoned—but that doesn't stop him from putting forth his best effort. These past few weeks, I've come to know him pretty well. I like him, and I respect him. He's a good person. Though he's trying to hide it beneath that attractive, stoic exterior, I can see he's torn up about you. So, I'm over here, wondering if I can help patch up things between you."

Marcel studied Anshu. "What did he tell you?"

"Nothing. He just pats my hand and tells me to focus on my work while he finds me the perfect alpha." Anshu flashed a smile. "Having you here is torture, and I'm not sure why he's doing this to himself."

Like it was full of lead, Marcel's gaze dropped to the floor. "It's my fault. I asked if he had a few minutes to talk, and he said he didn't. So I followed him. I thought he was going to work, and I'd just sit in the lobby or outside his office until he was ready to see me. I didn't think he'd let me get on a plane with him."

Anshu patted Marcel's hand and *tsked*. "Honey, if he didn't want you here, you wouldn't be here."

Marcel had figured as much. He didn't understand Zeke's motivation either.

"Sometimes it helps to talk to another omega," Anshu prompted. "Whatever you tell me will stay between us."

Something about Anshu Bray invited confidence. Marcel sighed. "My parents are lawyers, and they expected me to follow in their footsteps. From the time I was little, they made this clear. For Halloween, they used to dress me up as a judge. For my seventh birthday, they got me a gavel, but I wanted a tutu. I lobbied them to put me into a ballet class. It took two years, but they finally caved."

Anshu frowned, no doubt waiting for what this had to do with Zeke.

"I loved it," Marcel continued. "When I'm in my leotard, I feel like I can do anything. They didn't understand, so they limited the time I was allowed to spend dancing. After high school, they sent me to a college known for churning out talented lawyers. It did not have a dance program. Those were the worst two years of my life. It got bad, really bad. I started drinking heavily and smoking pot. I tried to kill myself twice."

Anshu's long fingers twined with Marcel's shorter ones. "You were depressed."

"Yeah. The second attempt landed me in the hospital, and I realized I'd given up the thing that meant the world to me in order to become someone I didn't want to be." Marcel ran a palm over his hair. "So I quit college and threw myself into dancing. My parents flipped out. They'd rather I take anti-depressants and stay in law school. When I came to Verdance, they cut me off financially. They still talk to me, but the only thing they'll buy me is a bus ticket home."

"And then Zane took your backpack, and you lost your job dancing in the theater." Anshu gasped. "That's horrible. I don't know what I'd do if I couldn't research and experiment. I love science the same way you love dance."

Happy that someone understood, Marcel turned toward his new friend. "But you're willing to give it all up to marry an alpha?"

"Hell, no." Anshu scoffed. "I won't give that up."

Marcel grinned. "Just like I won't give up dance. Once my ankle is healed, I'm going back onstage. Nobody is going to stop me."

Then he remembered that a little someone might do just that. He or she wouldn't be doing it on purpose, but the outcome would be the same.

Anshu waited a beat, and his smile slowly morphed to a frown. "What does that have to do with Zeke and being his omega? Did he say you'd have to give up dancing?"

"No," Marcel admitted. He had no intention of giving Zeke an opportunity to refuse to let him be himself. There was no way he could live without dance at the center of his life. Dread killed the joy he might have felt toward the bundle growing inside his body. "But I know how these things work. He'll want me to have kids and stay home to raise them."

Waving, Anshu dismissed Marcel's concern. "That's only for like fifteen or twenty years. You have plenty of time to dance after that."

Marcel gaped. "Nobody is going to hire a middle-aged dancer. If I have kids now, I'm throwing away my whole life."

Anshu considered this. "I forgot about the short lifespan of canine shifters. Dragons frequently live for five hundred years." He tapped a finger against his lower lip. "I wonder if carrying a hybrid fetus changes anything with regard to the omega's lifespan? It's worth considering whether it changes an omega's DNA."

The dragon omega's musings quieted until they were only inside his head. As he watched, Marcel wondered if Zeke had considered the problem that Marcel's lifespan wasn't as long as his. Did it bother him, or did it make him view Marcel as a temporary inconvenience?

"Can I get a DNA sample from you?" Without waiting for a response, Anshu hurried to where he'd stowed his bag. He returned with a sterile cheek swab kit. "Open up."

"Why do you want my DNA?"

"Research. I'm studying shifter genetics." He motioned for Marcel to open his mouth.

Marcel complied.

Anshu scraped the swab along the inside of Marcel's cheek. "Awesome. This will help, I hope."

"Help with what?"

"With understanding why I'm the last surviving dragon omega." Anshu pressed his lips together as he bagged and labeled the sample. "You see, dragon shifters are going extinct. I hope by studying our DNA and that of other shifters who aren't going extinct, I can find out what's causing there to be primarily alpha births, though even those are fewer and farther between. From an evolutionary perspective, you'd think there would be more omegas than alphas."

Marcel knew nothing about the topic. "You're seriously the last omega dragon?"

"I am." He pursed his lips. "You'd think they'd be lining up at my door to take me out, but they're not. The connection you have with Zeke is increasingly rare among our kind. In the last two decades, dragon alphas have been mating with omegas from domesticated species only—canine, feline, equine."

"Interesting," Marcel muttered. He appreciated how Anshu was taking his mind off his problems. "So, are you going to meet alphas who are canine, feline, or equine shifters?"

"No. I'm meeting a dragon from the Silver-Winged Tribe." Gears moved behind Anshu's eyes. "Of course, it stands to reason that if alphas aren't clicking with dragon omegas, then dragon omegas probably won't connect with dragon alphas. It'll be interesting to see how today's meeting goes."

To Marcel's way of thinking, flying to Miami was an awful long way to go for a blind date. "Have you video-chatted with him?"

"No. Dragons are primal creatures. Nothing will happen unless we're face-to-face."

That's how it had been with Zeke. The moment he'd walked into the room, Marcel's canine had awoken in a way it never had before. Where Zeke was concerned, Marcel was an uncontrolled mess.

Chapter 8

Zeke

Having Marcel in close proximity was killing him by degrees. His dragon wanted to shift, pick up the reluctant omega, and take him someplace private. Without the world to bother them, he might stand a chance at convincing Marcel they belonged together.

The café he'd chosen for Anshu's meeting with Kian Snow of the Silver-Winged Tribe was an open-air affair, which did not suit Zeke. The temperature in Miami was far too warm. He was used to winters high in the mountains, and he preferred cooler weather. In his rush to leave, he'd forgotten to bring a change of clothing. He could have done with some air conditioning.

Of course, the sexy omega waiting in his living room might have occupied his mind more than being prepared for midday in southern Florida.

He shrugged out of his jacket and loosened his tie.

Tito eyed him dispassionately. "You should have worn a lighter material."

Zeke opted not to reply.

Next to him, Marcel sipped an iced tea. He seemed preoccupied with watching Anshu and Kian having iced coffees on the other side of the café. That suited Zeke just fine. It meant Marcel wasn't looking at him, which meant he didn't have to spend his time trying to figure out what Marcel was thinking.

The omega wanted to talk to him.

He'd followed him all the way to Miami with nary a protest.

What could he have to say that was so important it couldn't wait, and did it have anything to do with the unknown thing nagging at Zeke's mind?

One thing Zeke knew for certain—Marcel hadn't changed his mind about having a relationship with him. He'd overheard him talking to Anshu on the plane, and he recognized the omega's resolve had nothing to do with him. It wasn't personal.

And that fucking sucked.

Marcel was his omega. It was personal to Zeke, and the hollow pain in his chest wasn't a feeling to which Zeke was accustomed, nor did he wish to be.

Across from him, Tito cleared his throat. "Ezekiel, now that I have you alone, relatively speaking, there's something important I want to talk to you about."

As head of security, Zeke was involved with many aspects of Draco International. Anything that needed or impacted security was his job to oversee. In some ways, he had more power than anyone else there, Tito included.

He masticated an ice cube. "Shoot."

For the first time since they'd met, Tito fidgeted in his seat. He tugged at his collar, which was already loose, and undid a third button. "When I made a deal with the Ice-Breathers to forge an alliance between our tribes, I didn't know Amaricio had found his omega. I though Edgar was just another fling, as you've all had flings with other kinds of omegas at one time or another. We all do it. I didn't know he was serious."

Zeke peered at Tito. "This sounds like a conversation you should be having with Amar."

"He won't talk to me about it."

"I don't know what you expect me to do." He'd tried talking to Grange about the matter, but his friend's mind was firmly made up. Now that he had an omega, albeit a reluctant one, Zeke understood Amaricio's vehement and volatile reaction.

"Nothing." Tito shook his head. "I'm trying to apologize to you, Ezekiel. I went about it all wrong. In hindsight, my moves look desperate. Perhaps they were. I deeply regret the actions I took and the way it has impacted our relationship. I had my reasons, and if you'll let me, I'd like to explain why I did what I did."

Zeke knew what had motivated Tito. It had come out at the trial, and it was the reason he'd been exonerated. His higher purpose had been to save dragonkind. On some level, it was a noble endeavor. It's just his execution of it had been wrong on so many levels. "That's not necessary."

"I believe it is."

"Fine." Now he understood what had really motivated Tito to come along on the trip. He'd wanted to confront Zeke when he was isolated and unable to leave. He was there to guard Anshu, and he couldn't leave the omega alone. He'd promised to keep him safe.

"When you and Amar were born after almost a hundred years of no births among our kind, you were heralded as miracles. But then you both turned out to be alphas, and no more babies have been born since. All breeding pairs are past their prime, and the chances they will reproduce again are not good." He sipped his cold drink.

Zeke did as well, and he noted that Marcel's attention had shifted to Tito. He was listening to the alpha's tale. Silently he waited for Tito to get past the retelling of things they both already knew and come to the point.

"I thought I was saving our kind with this deal. I'd met Anshu, and I thought his temperament more suited to Amaricio. He needs someone to take care of him, who understands his obsessive nature, who perhaps sets down rules so he doesn't work all hours of the day and night. You're not the kind of person who does that. You're more likely to build him a lab in your house than to restrict his activities."

If Anshu had been his, and he'd wanted a workspace at home, Zeke would have built him an office. He didn't think an experimental space would be safe in the home, but he could see where a place to work on the research aspects would be desirable. "You're forgetting Anshu didn't connect with Amar."

Tito acknowledged the truth of the matter. "No, he didn't. But sometimes a relationship is built on time and effort instead of an instant chemical reaction. In almost four hundred years, I have not had an instant connection with anyone."

Zeke glanced to Marcel. He wasn't sure he was a fan of the instant connection phenomenon. So far, for him, it had sucked.

"I'm sorry, Ezekiel. I meant well, for all of you and for all of dragonkind. I never meant to hurt you, and I certainly never meant to damage our relationship the way I have." Tito folded his hands on the table. It wasn't so much a power move as it was an indication he was waiting for Zeke to respond.

Before Zeke could say anything, Marcel snorted, the sound rich with disgust. "Seriously? You're apologizing without apologizing? You did some bad shit to Edgar, and you're talking about it like it was just a misunderstanding."

For the first time since that morning, Zeke looked directly at Marcel. It was like looking into the sun—beautiful and terrible all at the same time. Marcel was a salve forever out of reach, and that made his pain all the worse. The clamor of opposing feelings knocked him speechless.

Tito did not have that problem. "You have no idea what you're talking about."

"Yes, I do. Edgar told me what you did to him, how you kidnapped him and held him prisoner while you did medical experiments on him." Marcel glanced at Zeke. "And now you're preying on Zeke's good nature, looking for a way back into the fold. You're manipulating him with your blasé explanation and a quasi-heartfelt apology. You're making excuses for your behavior. The fact of the matter is that there is no excuse for what you did to Zeke. You treated him like dirt. He was good to you, loyal and kind, and you rejected him and treated him badly. And why? Because you're afraid of change. You're afraid of anything that's different from the way you thought your life should turn out."

With that, Marcel sprang to his feet, knocking his chair backward, and he left the café. Zeke twisted to watch him walk away. He wasn't sure if he was supposed to go after the enigmatic omega. "I wonder what that was about?"

Tito made a thoughtful noise. "I'm gathering from the fact that you've been giving him the silent treatment all day that, like me, he's not in your good graces at the moment. I'm guessing at least part of his outburst referred to himself and not to me." He tapped the table, drawing Zeke's attention back to the matter at hand. "I'm fully aware of what I did and how it hurt each of you. He's right that I chose to approach you first because you tend not to hold a grudge. You're generally reasonable, and you often forgive people even when they're not deserving. It's not that you're a pushover; it's that you have the ability to see beyond the small things to figure out what really matters."

Zeke had never heard himself described quite that way. He could be hard and exacting, and he was highly practical. Holding grudges was Amaricio's thing, not his. He longed to forgive Tito. He longed to mend his relationship with the man who'd meant so much to him for so many years.

He got to his feet slowly, cursing the hot temperatures as the move put him directly in the sun. "Tito, our relationship will never be what it was. You can't be my mentor, but perhaps you can be my friend. It'll take time."

Tito beamed. "We have time. Now, go after your omega. He went east on the next street over."

Zeke glanced toward Anshu. "Watch over him."

"I will."

Marcel

Shades of humiliation washed over him as he walked stiffly away from Zeke and Tito. He'd stuck his foot deep down his throat, and now he was hoping for an alien spaceship to swoop down and abduct him to save him from having to go back there. Every single time he talked around Zeke Lowry, it ended badly. Never in his life had Marcel been so bad at communication. When Zeke Lowry was around, Marcel's brain went on hiatus. It reverted to instinct and fear, and Marcel had some deep-seated fears that defied reason.

He ducked into a mostly deserted alley. Passing the huge metal trash cubes reeking of rotting produce, he found a loading bay that wasn't being used. He climbed onto the concrete dock, weaving himself neatly through the metal bars that served as a handrail and a way to stop anyone from accidentally falling off.

Sitting on the dock, he rested his arms on the lower bar and put his head in his hands. This wasn't how he'd planned for his day to go at all.

Anyone else who found themselves on an unexpected trip to a tropical location with the man of their dreams would have used the time to strengthen the bond between alpha and omega. Not only was Marcel terrified at the idea, but he was also frightened he was going to lose Zeke forever.

Zeke was the kind of man who listened to his words and gave him what he wanted. He'd stayed away because that's where Marcel had wanted him. Only now he had to face the fact he didn't want Zeke away from him at all.

The opposing needs pummeled his head, leaving him with a thundering between his ears that threatened his sanity.

"Is this seat taken?"

Marcel opened his eyes to see Zeke swing himself onto the dock and take the place next to him. Though they didn't touch, the fact of Zeke's close proximity automatically calmed the worst of Marcel's nerves.

"You know, Tito has been my mentor since I was a child. For a long time, he was like a third father to me. But I'm not a child anymore, and I've become adept at my job. The dynamics of our relationship were destined to change eventually."

Messages received. "I shouldn't have said anything. I'm sorry."

Zeke chuckled. "That's not what I meant. He did some horrible things, which forced me to retaliate, and it damaged our relationship. What we have now is something fractured and broken, but if we're both committed to putting it back together, we'll build something stronger. It'll be different, but that's not always a bad thing."

"I'm glad for you. It's hard when you can't talk to someone who has been like a father to you." Marcel would know. When he'd put his foot down with his fathers regarding his career choice, it had put distance between them. While he would love to bridge the gap, he couldn't see a way to repair it.

His relationship with Zeke suffered from the same missteps.

Missteps. Ha. More like hand grenades.

"I have time to talk to you now. What did you want to say to me?" Next to him, Zeke stiffened, as if girding himself for the coming attack.

Marcel shrugged. "It doesn't seem important anymore."

"You got in my cab, waited at my house, then flew halfway across the country, and now you've decided it's not important?"

He'd decided it was stupid. He'd planned to apologize and explain, to make excuses for what he'd done to Zeke—same as what Tito had done. When he'd heard the older man speak, it had struck him that excuses were hollow, and they didn't excuse anything. Actions mattered.

Right now, he had no idea what actions to take.

He waited, but Zeke settled into the silence.

Finally, he sighed. "I listened to what Tito said to you, how he made excuses for what he did as part of his apology." He broke off, searching for elusive words.

Zeke waited with a patience Marcel could only envy.

Taking a deep breath, he blurted a confession. "I was going to do that. I was going to apologize for the way I've treated you, and then I was going to explain why I said what I said. And then, when I heard Tito do the same thing, I realized it doesn't matter. I did what I did, and I said what I said, and no apology is going to take that back. So what if I panicked and phrased things badly? I was mean to you. I was horribly selfish and self-centered. I didn't think about you at all, only how being your omega would ruin my dreams. Nothing I can say now is going to take back what I said or erase the ways I've hurt you. You didn't deserve to be treated the way I've treated you. For fuck's sake, Zeke— you've been nothing but kind to me. And patient. And understanding. I don't deserve someone like you in my life."

At that moment, Marcel realized, despite his best effort, he'd fallen head-over-heels for a man who had every right to hate him. It was more than primal, animal attraction. He genuinely liked Zeke, and he wanted desperately to have him in his life.

Zeke's gaze roamed the plain brick facing of the rear of the buildings that surrounded them. He seemed lost in thought. After ten tense moments passed, he nodded. "An honest apology means something. It means you're sorry for what you did and you regret that it happened at all. It means if you had the chance to do it again, you'd do it differently. Tito meant what he said. He didn't apologize for the parts he wasn't sorry about, and frankly, I didn't expect him to. I didn't disagree with his intention, only his execution."

The man's capacity for forgiveness was incredible, though Marcel considered what he'd done to Zeke was worse. "Well, I'm glad you two are working things out."

"Yeah. We'll see how that goes. It's not so much that I'm holding a grudge as it is that Amaricio isn't going to let it go. My loyalty was divided, but now that I've met you, I understand the depth of Amar's anger and sense of betrayal." Zeke's gaze swept the area again, and this time it landed on Marcel. "The things you said to me were cruel. I'm not going to pretend it doesn't matter. An explanation would go a long way toward helping me understand why you rejected me from the start and lashed out at me so vehemently."

"It won't excuse what I've done," Marcel warned.

"It's easier to forgive what I understand." Zeke flashed a small, sad smile.

Marcel exhaled hard. He could grant Zeke's request. "My fathers are lawyers, and they raised me to be one too. For my first Halloween, they dressed me up as a judge. When I was seven, we went to a matinee performance of Oklahoma at the community theater in my hometown. I was entranced from the moment the curtain rose. For weeks afterward, I danced around the house, recreating the musical the best I could by myself. It took me almost two years to convince my fathers to let me take a dance class. They didn't really understand, but they indulged me in one dance class each semester."

He had wanted to take many more classes, but they'd refused to let him fill his afternoons and weekends with practices and shows. He'd spent a lot of time sneaking out to practice alone.

"In college, I majored in pre-law. The first year, I snuck in a dance class each semester at the local community theater. The second year, my fathers found out and stopped me from wasting my time on frivolous pursuits. I became depressed. I skipped classes, drank too much, smoked pot—anything that had the smallest chance of chasing away the sadness that felt like an elephant sitting on my chest. Six months ago, I tried for a second time to kill myself by taking a lot of pills."

He hadn't taken nearly enough. They'd fed him charcoal in the emergency room, and he'd gone home a few hours later.

"After that, I took stock of my life. I didn't want to be a lawyer. I wanted to be a dancer. Nothing makes me feel more free and alive than being up on stage, performing my heart out. So I moved out on my own, and I took any classes offered at the theater. I danced in a few productions, enough to land an audition at the Verdance Theater. Then I worked to save up enough to get to Verdance." He smiled as he remembered the elation of landing his first dancing role. Then it faded. "My fathers don't understand. They still talk to me, but they won't come out to see me perform. They say I'm wasting my potential. Every time I talk to them, they offer to buy me a bus ticket back there. They say they'll pay for me to finish my degree and go to law school. Yesterday they even offered to pay for me to be an engineer. I don't fit their idea of what they want me to be."

Zeke's gaze didn't waver. He watched Marcel intently, as if everything he said mattered.

It gave him the courage to continue. "When I was in the hospital, I vowed that, if I survived, I wasn't going to let anybody get between me and my dreams. I never thought I'd meet someone who made my poodle whimper. It's not a thing with canines. We don't have predetermined mates or anything. You meet someone you like, you date, and then you get married. Divorce is as common among canine shifters as it is among humans. The moment I met you, I knew that's not how it was with you."

"No," Zeke confirmed. "Dragons mate for life. When we meet our mate, it's a primal connection. Our animal knows before our human side does, and it doesn't negotiate. It doesn't acknowledge reason or circumstance."

"My canine side is behaving that way, and it's like nothing I've ever experienced. I panicked because I knew an alpha who is as big and strong and authoritative as you wouldn't have patience for what I wanted."

Zeke huffed and lifted his eyes in search of even more patience. "You assume facts not in evidence."

The unexpected law joke evoked a chuckle from Marcel. "I see the way Edgar serves Amar. He does everything for his alpha. And, you know what? I can see myself doing that for you. I can see me quitting dance and devoting myself to being your omega. I can also see myself waking up one day and realizing I'm monumentally unhappy."

Unimpressed, Zeke said, "Edgar was Amar's personal assistant before they got married. His job was to take care of Amar's personal life, which he never stopped doing. He even tries to take care of other people's personal lives. That's just who he is. Chay, the omega who married my friend Koren, works a couple nights each week tending bar. They don't need the money, but Chay enjoys it. Marcel, I'd never take dance away from you. That was an unfair assumption."

Ashamed, Marcel dropped his gaze to stare at the stained concrete below the dock. "I'm sorry for that. I'm sorry for lashing out at you and for saying horrible things to you."

"You were terrified I'd take you back to a dark time when you made decisions based on what people who loved you wanted for you rather than what you wanted for yourself." Zeke set his hand on top of Marcel's. "You didn't know me."

"I didn't give myself a chance to know you." Despite that, he had come to know Zeke.

"It's in your power to change that."

Marcel studied Zeke's hand on his, the lighter skin contrasting with his milk chocolate color. They were so very different—in temperament, personality, and experience—but perhaps that was for the best. A mercurial, reactive person like Marcel needed a mate who kept his wits about him and who was thoughtful in his responses.

His heart beat faster as he decided to take a chance. "You'd be willing to forgive me?"

"I think it's best if we start over."

"I'd like that." Joy lit Marcel from the inside.

Chapter 9

Zeke

In one day, two important people who'd wronged him had apologized. Zeke was flying high, living amongst the stars. Exhilarated, he pulled Marcel to him and captured his lips in a searing kiss that went on and on.

When it ended, he pressed his forehead to Marcel's. "Hello, omega. I'm Zeke Lowry, and I'd like to take you on a date."

Marcel laughed, a rich, musical sound. "Hi, Zeke Lowry. I'm Marcel, and I'd love to go out on a date with you. I'm free tomorrow night."

Zeke didn't want to wait that long. "How about tonight? We can send Tito and Anshu back to Verdance, and we can fly back tomorrow."

"I didn't bring a change of clothes."

"Miami is full of stores. I'll buy anything you need." Zeke wanted to spoil Marcel. He wanted to shower him with gifts, to show him that as long as they were together, anything was possible.

A hint of heat permeated Marcel's skin, and Zeke sensed, more than saw, evidence of his omega's discomfort. "That's not necessary."

"But it's fun." Zeke swung down from the dock. "We need to get back. Tito has trouble sitting back and letting events unfold naturally. I need to make sure he isn't pressuring Anshu or Kian into something neither of them wants."

Marcel hopped down, and Zeke snatched him out of the air.

"Nice reflexes."

"I didn't want you to reinjure your ankle," he explained. "You haven't started physical therapy yet."

"Thank you."

Though he wanted to take Marcel's hand on the walk back to the café, Zeke refrained. His omega was emotional and given to rash reactions. He didn't want to damage the fragile beginnings of trust they'd established between them.

Back at the café, he found Tito where he'd left him. He sat down, and Marcel resumed his seat as well.

Tito studied them both, his gaze roaming Marcel before returning to Zeke. "You worked things out. That's great."

For the first time, Tito sounded as if he meant the sentiment. It seemed he was coming to accept the fact alpha dragons were being drawn to omegas from more domesticated species.

Zeke didn't know anything about genetics; he only knew what his dragon wanted. He faced Tito. "I'm sending you and Anshu home tonight. Marcel and I will return tomorrow."

Tito considered this. Wheels churned behind his eyes, and he rubbed his hands together. "Let's all stay the night. It's been a long time since I've been to Miami. I have a friend who lives nearby. I'd like to spend some time with her."

Now that they'd outed Tito, he was less secretive about his liaisons with women.

Zeke unlocked his phone. "I'll make reservations at a hotel."

Ten minutes later, he had confirmation numbers for Tito and Anshu, and he'd booked a suite for Marcel and him. It would keep Marcel close, but it would afford him distance and privacy if that's what he wanted.

He'd also used his connections from his position at Draco International to score tickets to a production of a show that had great reviews. He'd never heard of it, but he was sure Marcel would appreciate the experience.

Four hours later, he met Marcel in the common room of their suite. His omega wore a cream colored suit with lemon pinstripes. He'd selected a sleek hat with wide brim that brought the entire ensemble together. Zeke took a moment to appreciate the way the cut hugged Marcel's muscular thighs and emphasized his package.

For his part, Zeke had stuck with his tried-and-true formula of a dark suit with a light shirt. Marcel went to Zeke, hands out, and straightened his tie.

"You look handsome, as always," Marcel said.

A sly smile tipped Zeke's mouth. He was not at all humble about his extreme good looks. "You're going to be the envy of every man there tonight."

Marcel choked out a laugh.

Zeke guided Marcel out of the room. "Did you have a snack? Our reservation is for ten-thirty."

Glancing back over his shoulder, Marcel frowned. "You don't have to take me somewhere that requires a reservation. I know this is all last-minute."

By way of response, Zeke flashed a cocky grin. "Cupcake, this is our first date. Everything will be perfect."

He'd half expected Marcel to object to his use of the nickname he'd hated before, but Marcel merely shook his head. "I suppose it's pointless for me to do anything but enjoy the date?"

"It is."

"What's Anshu doing tonight?"

"He's out with Kian. He said they didn't make a love connection, but there's a mutual attraction, and they're both willing to give it a shot." Zeke knew from talking with Koren that Anshu wanted to have sex. The omega was still a virgin, and he wanted to lose that status quickly. If Kian was interested, then both shifters would have a happy ending to the night.

"At least nobody is sitting in a hotel room alone."

Later that night, when Marcel's eyes were still sparkling with excitement from the show, Zeke brought him back to their suite. It had two bedrooms because he didn't want Marcel to feel obligated to have sex.

In the living room, he kissed Marcel. He kept the pressure light, and he concentrated on a sensual experience. Before they got carried away, he broke the connection.

Marcel clutched Zeke's shirt, holding him close. "I have a confession to make."

Prepared for Marcel to ask him to take it slowly, Zeke rested his hands on his omega's hips. "You want to sleep in your own room tonight."

Marcel's mouth opened and closed as he frowned. "I'm not asking you to guess. I'm going to speak plainly."

Though the date had gone well, he braced himself nonetheless.

"I'm pregnant."

The moment Zeke processed the statement, he realized he already knew. This had been the thing gnawing at the edge of his consciousness since the day before. He'd noted Marcel's rounded abdomen, but he hadn't thought about what it meant.

"Zeke, say something. I'm freaking out over here."

"It happened that first night." He gripped Marcel's hips a little tighter, drawing his omega's body closer. "When we were both out of our minds with passion."

"Yeah," Marcel confirmed. "And I had a concussion. I was definitely not thinking clearly."

A series of emotions zinged through Zeke, all of them degrees of elation. Then he realized this was exactly what Marcel was afraid would happen. His omega was freaking out, not only in anticipation of Zeke's reaction, but of how this will affect his life. "We can do this, Marcel. I promise it'll all work out. You can be my omega, be a dad, and also have your career. I know nothing about kids, but I'll learn. And we can get a nanny for when we're at work. "

He pictured himself wearing one of those baby slings over his suit and carrying his child around with him at work. The nanny could stick around for when Zeke had a meeting or needed to go somewhere that wasn't baby-friendly.

Draco International needed a child care center. In his mind, he was already converting the conference room on the third floor into an infant care room. Next to that, they'd have something for toddlers.

A sob jerked him from the daydream.

Marcel buried his face in Zeke's chest. Automatically, Zeke's arms came up and wrapped around his omega. "It's okay, Marcel. I know it's not the way you wanted your life to unfold, but it's not the end of the world. I'm here. I'm not going anywhere. I'll always be here for you. I'll always take care of you."

"I know that now, but it's just... I just... For the past month, I've been thinking I would have to give up the baby or my dreams."

"No," Zeke interrupted. "You're gaining an alpha and a baby. You're not giving up anything."

"I like your house," Marcel whispered. "It's not decorated like a bordello."

"What? Who said it was decorated like a bordello?"

Marcel lifted his tear-streaked face to meet Zeke's gaze. "Nobody. Edgar was rambling, but he wasn't talking about your house."

Edgar was given to rambling, so Zeke moved on to important things. "I'm glad you like my house because it's ours now. I'll convert the basement into a dance studio for you, and we'll put a nursery on the second floor."

A small, shy smile lifted Marcel's luscious lips. "When I met you, I was terrified my life was over, but now I can see that it's just beginning."

Zeke kissed his omega with all the affection in his heart, and then he carried him to the bedroom where he made tender love to him.

Epilogue

Marcel

Iron bands squeezed his midsection, and they were nothing like the comforting familiarity of Zeke's arms.

He doubled over and groaned before he remembered to breathe through it. Meanwhile, he fumbled for his phone and dialed Zeke's number. "It's time," he gasped when his alpha answered.

"I'll be home in two minutes."

The call disconnected, which meant Zeke was now in dragon form and flying high over the city to take the direct route home. The contraction eased, and Marcel made his way up the stairs. By the time he arrived, Zeke was there. Having landed on the balcony off the bedroom, he hadn't needed to navigate the stairs.

He shimmied into a pair of jeans, and then he swept the covers off the bed and put on the waterproof birthing cover. "Do you need help taking off your pants?"

Now that the first contraction was in the past, Marcel felt fine. "Maybe it was a false alarm?"

Zeke glanced over, mischief lighting his blue eyes. "Take your pants off anyway. If it was a false alarm, then I'm going to make the most out of leaving a meeting to rush home to be with my sexy omega."

In the past month, Zeke had proven to be an insatiable lover. Not a day passed that Marcel wasn't the target of a cunning charm offensive. Only three hours ago, he'd awoken to Zeke's lips on his neck and his alpha's hand on his ass. Then he'd come down the stairs to find roses on the kitchen counter.

The dance studio in the basement was nearly complete, and the nursery had been ready for two whole days. Zeke was a man of his word. He made sure Marcel went to physical therapy, and he'd invited Scylla and other important theater people over to the house for dinner several times.

Marcel slid out of the loose sweats he'd borrowed from Zeke. The soft fabric fluttered to the floor, and he stepped out of them. Giving Zeke his most inviting smile, Marcel took one step closer.

That's when another contraction hit. Nope, not a false alarm.

Zeke caught him, lifting him easily to deposit him on the bed. He propped pillows under Marcel's shoulders. "Have you settled on a name?"

Prenatal scans showed a single birth, and they had prepared to welcome a little girl into the world.

Marcel concentrated on breathing. "Sofia, with an *f*, not a *ph*."

"I like it." Zeke grinned. The name had been his lone suggestion on a list that included over twenty names. The grin remained in place as put on a shirt and set a nylon bag on the dresser. Koren had given it to him. The bag would stay around his neck when he was in dragon form, and it held small items, like his wallet, phone, and keys.

Zeke's phone rang. Without dimming his smile, he answered. "Chay? What's up? The raccoon is in the butterfly bush? What the hell does that mean?"

As he rolled up his sleeves and listened, he shot Marcel a questioning glance, but Marcel merely lifted his shoulder.

"Oh!" Zeke straightened up. "You know where the thief is? That's great, but I can't come now. Marcel is in labor. Call the police and ask for Marcie Mavensburg. She'll take care of it. What? Not now. I'll call when Sofia is born."

He ended the call and tossed his phone toward a table near the bed. It landed on the floor with a clatter, but Zeke didn't seem to care.

"Chay found the man who stole Zane's backpack, and I told him not to have people come over until after the baby is born."

They both knew visitors would start showing up any minute. Edgar would be among the first wave, and he'd put himself in charge of everyone else who came.

"Have you called your fathers yet?" Zeke's tone was gentle and nonjudgmental.

Marcel sighed. He hadn't told his fathers he was married, pregnant, or that he'd been injured. "Let's worry about them later."

Zeke opened his mouth to argue, but another contraction hit. He pushed Marcel's knees up and out of the way. "The opening is forming, so it won't be long now."

"They're going to pressure me to stay home with the baby or go to law school."

"I'm your alpha, and I'm not going to let you do either thing."

They'd had this discussion before. Zeke supported paternity leave for both of them, but he insisted Marcel would be back in the theater by the following summer, six months away. He thought he could get Marcel's fathers to back off, and Marcel loved him for his optimism.

"Zeke?"

"Yeah, cupcake?"

Laughing at the nickname he initially hadn't liked, Marcel said, "Sofia is coming right now."

Zeke hurried into position. Another set of contractions hit, and Marcel pushed as Zeke murmured praise and support. With a gush of fluids, Sofia Lowry entered the world. Beaming with joy and pride, Zeke held the tiny baby against his ruined shirt. "Hello, Sofia. I'm your father, and I'm going to love you and take care of you. Whenever you need anything, I'll be there for you."

Then he placed Sofia onto Marcel's chest.

"Say hello to your daddy, sweetheart."

Joy and love swelled in his heart. Marcel took in his daughter's delicate features. She had a shock of dark hair to go with her dark skin. Her mouth opened in a cute O, and a second later she let loose with a loud squall.

"Shh, Sofia. You're okay. I've got you."

While Zeke took care of the afterbirth, Marcel cleaned up his daughter with a warm cloth. When he wrapped her in a soft blanket, she quieted. For the first time, she opened her eyes, and she gazed at Marcel with brilliant blue eyes, an exact replica of Zeke's.

"She has your eyes," he said softly.

Sofia resumed fussing.

Zeke chuckled. "And your temperament. I think she's hungry. Being born is hard work."

"Yes." Marcel lifted his shirt and nursed his little girl. "It's very hard work, and she did great."

Zeke settled on the bed next to Marcel and watched them both. "So did you. Have I told you lately how much I love you?"

"Not since this morning." Marcel tore his gaze from the miracle in his arms. "I love you too."

Zeke pressed a kiss to Marcel's lips. "Thank you for this."

Marcel beamed as he snuggled into Zeke's embrace. They stayed like that for a while, luxuriating in the love of their family and watching the newest member replenish her energy.

A knock at their bedroom door had Zeke chuckling. He tucked a blanket around Marcel's lower half. "It's safe to come in, Edgar."

The door opened, and Edgar crept through. "It's quiet. Is she already asleep?"

"She's eating," Marcel said. "Come see her."

Edgar oohed and aahed over Sofia for a few minutes, and then he set a hand on Zeke's shoulder. "Chay called. They arrested the guy who stole Zane's backpack. It's a ring responsible for a whole bunch of small thefts going back two years. The Verdance PD is going to honor Chay with a ceremony and a plaque."

Zeke chuckled. "I'd like to honor the thief with a ceremony and a plaque for bringing Marcel into my life, but good for Chay. I'm happy for him."

"Also, Marcel's phone rang when I was downstairs, and I answered it because the display said it was his father."

Marcel groaned. "Please tell me you didn't say anything about me having a baby."

Color crept up Edgar's neck. "I didn't know you were estranged. I told them you were in labor and your husband was handling the delivery. Your father cried. They're on their way here."

Zeke looked from Sofia to Marcel. "I can't imagine not being part of her life, Marcel. I can't help but think your fathers feel the same way about you."

"I guess we'll see." He groaned again. When he opened his eyes, he found Zeke watching him.

"I'll be by your side the whole time," Zeke promised. "No matter what, you have me in your corner."

"Which means you'll be fine," Edgar added. "Because Zeke is badass. Hey, she's done eating. Can I hold her? Please, please, please? I already love my little niece so much."

Marcel looked to Zeke, not because he was his alpha, but because he might be feeling territorial about his daughter.

Zeke nodded. "For a minute, and then she's mine." He glanced at Marcel. "I may never let her go, so Edgar got here at a good time."

As Edgar rocked Sofia in his arms, Zeke moved closer to Marcel. "I meant it, cupcake. I'll always be here for you, even when you don't want me."

Marcel buried his face in his alpha's neck. "I always want you here with me. Haven't you realized that I've accepted my fate? I love you, Zeke. Always."

Zeke pressed a kiss to Marcel's head and hugged him tighter.

About A. J. Stone

A.J. Stone loves rainbows and bears. Visit https://michelezurloauthor.com/a-j-stone/ for the latest information or follow on Facebook at https://www.facebook.com/AJStoneBearsCove/ to keep up with the newest releases, and feel free to request stories for your favorite Bear's Cove characters.

Reviews let A.J. know you want more!

Bear's Cove Series (MM/MPreg) by A. J. Stone

Dak's Omega
Tanzil's Second Chance
Perfect Blend: Kofi's Omega

Draco International Series (MM/MPreg) by A. J. Stone

Amaricio's Omega Shifter
Koren's Omega Neighbor
Zeke's Reluctant Omega

MM Romance by Nicoline Tiernan

Nexus #1: Tristan's Lover by Nicoline Tiernan
Nexus #2: The Man of His Dreams by Nicoline Tiernan

Sneak Peek at Dak's Omega

Nerves randomly fired in Chase's body, making him feel off-kilter as he entered Dak's house. He should have come straight here from work. Beneath his greasy mechanic's coveralls, his clothes had been in fine shape. Except they smelled like the garage, and Dak had seemed strangely distant when he'd come by.

Dak's fingertips were a gentle pressure on Chase's lower back. "Are you hungry?"

This wasn't a date. No matter what kind of mixed signals he was getting from Dak, the last one had been clear—he wasn't flirting. Of course, Dak hadn't flirted at all. In flashes and moments, there had been hints of desire, the chemical pull of attraction, and that spanking. The skin on Chase's ass heated just from the memory.

This wasn't a date—except Dak had changed into jeans that made the bulge at the apex of his thighs look that much larger and a shirt that emphasized his wide shoulders and strong chest. The short sleeves strained to cover Dak's massive biceps.

Chase leaned into the hand on his back, turning to face Dak. Inches separated them. He held up the key to the patrol car. "I brought these."

Dak's clear blue gaze didn't acknowledge the statement. Wordlessly he demanded a response.

"I'm hungry." He didn't specify exactly what he was craving. Though whatever was in the oven smelled scrumptious, Chase wanted to taste something else. Right now, he wanted another kiss from the deputy. Not one to wait for what he wanted, Chase rose to his toes and pressed his lips to Dak's. It was an offering, and his heart pounded so hard he thought it might burst out of his chest.

Dak's fingertips slid to Chase's waist, the pressure increasing until his grip was firm. Dak's tongue traced along Chase's lower lip, and Chase opened to this gentle request.

Once he did that, all bets were off. Dak gripped the back of Chase's neck, tilting his head to let Dak's tongue inside. With his kiss, he ravaged Chase's mouth and liquefied his bones.

www.ingramcontent.com/pod-product-compliance
Lightning Source LLC
Chambersburg PA
CBHW030600130626
46552CB00006B/2615